GUNNER
A Lords of Carnage MC Romance

DAPHNE LOVELING

Copyright © 2017 Daphne Loveling

All rights reserved.

ISBN-13:
978-1976245589

ISBN-10:
1976245583

This book is a work of fiction.

Any similarity to persons living or dead is purely coincidental.

Cover design: Coverlüv
Cover image: SIBAShouse/Shutterstock.com

CONTENTS

1	Gunner	1
2	Alix	8
3	Gunner	19
4	Alix	25
5	Gunner	35
6	Alix	47
7	Gunner	56
8	Alix	63
9	Alix	69
10	Gunner	77
11	Alix	85
12	Gunner	92
13	Alix	102
14	Gunner	109
15	Alix	116
16	Gunner	124
17	Alix	137
18	Alix	149
19	Gunner	161

20	Alix	170
21	Gunner	181
22	Alix	193
23	Gunner	201
24	Gunner	211
25	Alix	221
26	Alix	227
27	Gunner	236
28	Alix	247
29	Gunner	254
30	Alix	262
31	Gunner	270
Epilogue	Alix	278
	Also by Daphne Loveling	289
	About the Author	291

To all the orphans.

1
GUNNER

"All right, fuckers," Beast says to Thorn and me as we grab our stools and sit down. "Which one of us is payin' for the first round?"

The three of us just arrived at the Smiling Skull, after a long ride on a late summer day. The Skull is a biker bar a few towns over from Tanner Springs — where we live, and where our club, the Lords of Carnage, is based. It's one of the few neutral territory biker bars in the area. Apart from the occasional bar fight, the Skull is a place where rival clubs come to drink in *mostly* peaceful coexistence. This uneasy truce is largely due to the vigilance of Rosie, the diminutive, brassy sixty-something woman who owns the place. She's barely five feet tall, and looks like she weighs less than my arm. But somehow, she manages to keep a bunch of huge, tattooed and drunken men from killing each other.

"I think it's your turn to pay, brother," Thorn smirks at

Beast with a gleam in his eye. "Seeing's how Gunner managed to beat your ass at arm wrestling back at the clubhouse earlier."

Beast's face turns instantly stormy. It's a look that would send most able-bodied men running for the damn exits. Beast is fucking huge, a monster at six-seven, and close to three-hundred pounds of solid muscle. It's a major coup that I managed to beat him arm wrestling. It's a feat no one else in the club has managed — and I'm not about to tell him or anyone else how I did it.

"He's right, brother," I nod, twisting the fork in just a little more and enjoying the hell out of it. "You owe me one. *At least* one."

Beast blows out a disgusted breath. "Fine. I'm buying. Goddamnit," he says gloomily.

"Jack and coke for me, spiked with vodka," I say, standing. "I'm gonna hit the head."

"Why the fuck do you gotta drink that vile mixture?" Beast complains. "Why can't you just drink a goddamn beer or a whiskey or something?"

"Who knows?" I grin at him. "Maybe that vile mixture is the secret to how I *beat your ass at arm wrestling.*"

"Fuck you, brother," Beast growls.

"Love you, too," I shoot back.

Thorn starts laughing uproariously as I make my way toward the back of the bar. Scanning the crowds as I move, I notice various clusters of men from most of the MCs around the area. Some of them raise a finger or lift their chin at me in greeting. A few others, from clubs we've pissed off in the past, glower and turn away from me. It's all good. Like I said, the Smiling Skull's neutral ground. And besides, it's still pretty early in the evening. Most fights start later on, when people are drunker and looking for a way to blow off steam.

One noticeable absence from the bar is any representation from the Iron Spiders. I make a mental note to mention this to Rock and the rest of the Lords of Carnage later. The Iron Spiders are — or *were* — an MC to the south of our territory in Tanner Springs. They were making some pretty serious attempts to fuck us over and destroy our club. They almost managed to inflict some serious damage. Until we took matters into our own hands and cut off the Spider's head, that is. We ended their president, Black, and took out a few of their other officers in the process. Ever since then, the Iron Spiders MC has gone completely underground. No one's seen hide nor hair of them in months, as far as we've been able to determine. Which may mean that the Iron Spiders are no more. Or it may mean they've gone silent while they regroup.

The second option is more likely.

And when they do, the Lords of Carnage will be waiting for them.

In the meantime, though, fuck 'em. I ain't about to look a

gift horse in the mouth. And the Iron Spiders being wiped off the map is one hell of a goddamn gift horse.

Inside the men's room, I take a much-needed piss and think of a couple other one-liners to roast Beast with. I'm already cracking myself up as I push the door open and walk back out into the bar. Across the room, I can tell that Thorn's regaling Beast with some bullshit story to try to cheer his ass up. I'd *almost* feel bad that I'm planning to go back over there and keep rubbing his nose in his defeat. If it wasn't gonna be so damn much fun, that is.

As I pass by the near end of the bar, the sound of an argument makes me turn my head. A high-pitched, angry voice pierces through the other noise in the room. It's a girl, probably in her early twenties. She must have just gotten here while I was in the head, because I can't imagine how I would have failed to notice her if she was here before that. She's about the furthest thing from a typical biker chick or club groupie I've ever seen in a bar like this. She's petite, not much taller than five-two or five-three. She's got shoulder-length wavy light blond hair that actually looks like it isn't a dye job. She's wearing a simple white T-shirt dress and flat sandals, and no makeup except for maybe some pale pink lipstick on her soft, full lips.

She literally looks like a breath of fresh air in this smoky, dingy dive. She sticks out like a sore thumb.

The chick is talking with a rough-looking guy who she can't possibly have come in here with. She's flailing her arms, looking agitated and frustrated as the guy shrugs his shoulders and takes a swig of his beer. She's a brave one, I'll give her that. He could crush her with one arm, if he had a mind to. As I pass by them, I can't tell what she's upset about, but I make out a couple of words.

"…Know where she is…"

"You can't… her away…"

Frowning, I mentally shrug and put it out of my mind. This shit is none of my business. People get up to all sorts of crazy-ass bullshit, and if this girl wants to hang out in a biker bar and argue with the local wildlife, that's fine by me.

I get back to my brothers and grab my seat. My jack and coke is sitting there, waiting for me. I lift the glass at Beast and Thorn.

"To Beast," I announce. "He may not be the strongest guy in the world, but he's still my brother."

"Goddamnit, Gun, are you gonna fucking let this go?" Beast explodes.

"Christ, I hope not," Thorn sputters, laughing so hard there are tears in his eyes. "This shite is priceless!"

"Sorry, brother, but Thorn's right," I chuckle. "It is pretty goddamn funny."

Eventually, I let Beast change the conversation, mostly so I can bring it up again when he's not expecting it. He and Thorn start shooting the shit about some biker wannabe they saw in town the other day who drove up on a tricked out rice burner, wearing so much Harley shit it looked like he bought out the whole store. "I mean, Christ, with all the shite he was wearing, he could have just used that money and put up a down payment on a *real* bike," Thorn says, shaking his head. "It was comical, though, I'll give him that."

I'm nodding and laughing along with them, stealing occasional looks at the blond chick at the other end of the bar. She's still arguing with the rough-looking dude. From behind, I can see the curve of her ass through the fabric of her dress, and the back of her shapely thighs, which look toned and muscled. I take a swig of my jack and coke, and think about how good it would feel to grab that ass and pull her onto my cock, sinking myself deep inside her. I imagine the sounds she'd make in her throat when I fisted my hands in her hair and started fucking her for all she's worth, and how her pussy would tighten around me as she came, right before I exploded inside her.

Jesus. I'm hard as a rock.

I try to pay attention to Beast and Thorn long enough to make my cock go back down, but the girl's a flash of light in an otherwise dark bar, and she's goddamn distracting. As I continue to cast glances in her direction, another guy joins them — of the same dirtbag stock as the first one. He's shaking his head and giving the girl a leering grin. Even from here I can he's being patronizing as fuck. Whatever she's mad about, they seem to find it more amusing than anything. Eventually she throws up her hands, sets down the beer she's been drinking, and stalks off in the direction of the bathrooms. The first dude leans over to the other one and says something to him that makes him laugh out loud.

Then, as I watch, the first dude slides his arm over toward the girl's beer and slips something small through the opening of the bottle.

Oh, *fuck* no.

There is no goddamn way someone is going to roofie a woman on my watch.

"Gentlemen," I mutter at Thorn and Beast. "I have a little business to attend to. Watch my six in case I need backup."

2
ALIX

Just when I thought things couldn't get worse than they already are, I come out of the bathroom of the Smiling Skull to see some guy punching Gonzalo.

Not that I really mind that part. Gonzalo is a freaking asshole. He deserves to be punched more than anyone I know. But right now, what I need from him is to tell me where the hell my sister is.

He knows. I *know* he does. But he's acting like he has no idea what I'm talking about. He doesn't even seem to give a damn whether I believe him or not. Which I guess he doesn't have to. I'm at least a foot shorter than him, and probably a hundred pounds lighter. I can't make him do a single thing. I don't even know why I came here in the first place, thinking I would ever be able to change any of this. Tears prick my eyes and sting my throat. I've never felt so helpless and alone in my life. And given the life I've had so far, that's saying something.

So, even though I came back out here to continue pleading with Gonzalo, I let myself have just a couple of seconds of pleasure and satisfaction watching the other guy land a blow to his face that sends him reeling backwards into a table.

"Fuck!" Gonzalo's asshole friend screams, and lurches toward the biker. Gonzalo's on the floor now, and so the biker easily has time to pivot, grab the second guy by the shirt, and launch him face first into the bar. His skull makes a sickening crack against the surface. I flinch and take a step back, instinctively reaching for my beer for something to hold in front of me. The bottle's cool and soothing in my hand. I take a long drink to calm my nerves, then wait to see what will happen next.

Gonzalo gets to his feet, rage in his eyes and blood on his lips. But before he can charge at the guy who hit him, two more men wearing the same patches on their leather vests are there. One, an enormous hulk of a man, grabs Gonzalo and pulls him backward so hard that he lifts him completely off his feet. The other, dark and handsome with a strong, square jaw, grabs Gonzalo's buddy by the neck and hauls him to his feet, his forehead bleeding profusely.

"If my brother punched you," the huge biker says to Gonzalo in a low, menacing tone, "it means you deserved it. So I'd advise against continuing this fight, unless you want to carry your teeth home in a bag."

"What the fuck?" splutters Gonzalo, blood and spittle flying from his mouth. "I've never seen this fucker before in my life!"

"Steady on, my friend," warns the other biker in a brogue I think is Irish.

No one is paying any attention to me at all, which is just fine by me. Watching Gonzalo get owned by a bunch of toughs is quite entertaining. I decide just to enjoy the show while it lasts.

"What the fuck did I ever do to you?" Gonzalo yells. "I'm serious! I have no fucking idea what the hell is going on!"

"You didn't do a goddamn thing to me," the first biker snarls. "But you know damn well what you did to the lady here."

I take another swig of my beer, finishing it, as they all turn to look at me.

The biker who punched Gonzalo's eyes lock on mine. Then they slide down to the now-empty bottle in my hand.

"Oh, shit," he groans.

* * *

"I am not going to stick my fingers down my throat," I protest as the biker pulls me toward the bathrooms. "What the hell is going on?"

"That fuckbag roofied you," he growls.

"What?" I ask in confusion. "You mean the *date rape drug?*"

"He slipped it into your beer when you were in the bathroom."

A thread of panic starts to weave itself up through my consciousness. "You mean, it's already in my system?" I cry.

"Not if you can get it out in time." He pushes on the door to the women's bathroom, but it's locked. He lifts his large fist and pounds on it so hard I'm afraid it will splinter. "Get the fuck out of there, *now!*" he yells.

A few moments later, a frightened looking woman in tight red leather comes tottering out. "Jesus, hold your horses!" she starts to complain, but goes silent when her eyes lock on the furious-looking biker. "Sorry," she squeaks, and skitters away. The man pulls me roughly through the door and locks it from the inside.

"Go on," he urges. "You don't have much time."

I have no idea how to do this. I know it's supposed to engage your gag reflex if you stick your fingers far enough down, but I've never tried it. Uncertainly, I stand in front of the toilet and lean over just a little, then stick my index finger inside my mouth until I touch the back of my throat. Instinctively, I recoil and start coughing. It's too hard; it'll never work.

"I can't do it," I wheeze.

"Yes you *can*," he bites out. "Do it, or I'll do it for you."

Ugh. Okay, having a total stranger — especially a very *hot* one, I'm starting to realize — stick his finger down my throat is *not* something I want to experience tonight. And judging from the fierce look on his bearded face, he's not kidding around. Gingerly, I stick my hand back in my mouth, close my eyes, and *ram* my fingers down my throat.

And promptly throw up all my beer into the toilet.

"Good girl," the biker growls as I gag and sputter. Some of the beer has gone up through my nose, and a little bit is running down my chin. *Gross.* I grab at the toilet paper dispenser, pulling off a long length, and blow my nose, mortified. Then I grab another length and wipe at my eyes, which are watering.

"Come on," the biker says. "Let's get you out of here. Did you come with anyone?"

"No," I gasp, and turn on the water in the sink. I cup my hands under the faucet, take a mouthful to rinse, and then another cup to drink. The third one, I splash on my face. "I came here alone."

I turn around to see him frowning disapprovingly. "You came to a biker bar by yourself?"

In spite of myself, I jut out my chin. "It's a free country."

He snorts. "Yeah. Free to be an idiot."

I resist the urge to tell him to fuck off, because after all, he did just save me from… *something*. Something definitely not good.

I shudder involuntarily.

Whatever he did just save me from, I can only imagine. Shit, has Gonzalo done this sort of thing before? People don't just *happen* to have roofies on them, after all. Not unless they plan to use them. Has Gonzalo done this to my sister?

Up until now, I've always assumed Eden went with Gonzalo of her own free will. The thought that maybe I was wrong is horrifying. I swallow a sob, my face crumpling into the beginnings of panic.

"Hey, Jesus, I'm sorry," the biker says, mistaking my look for hurt at his remark. "Look, though. Seriously, you shouldn't be in a place like this. You look like a nice girl. You gotta be more careful."

"I have my reasons," I insist stubbornly. "I didn't come here for fun."

"Yeah? What are they?" One brow goes up as he stares at me pointedly.

For the first time, I take a moment to really look at his face as I try to think what to respond. He's actually incredibly handsome. His hair is close-cropped. His dark beard only serves to accentuate the strong, square jaw beneath. Piercing blue eyes bore into me from under thick brows. Intricate tattoos cover the muscles on his arms. Even here in this gross bathroom, the guy pretty much radiates raw sexual power. I'm suddenly very aware that we're in this tiny room all alone.

And that if we were anywhere else but a filthy dive bar restroom, I'd be hoping maybe he'd do something about it.

"It's none of your business why I'm here," I say uncertainly, my voice quavering. "Thank you very much for helping me. But I think I should leave now."

"Yeah. You should," he agrees, and reaches to open the bathroom door. I walk through it, trying to keep my head high and not look like someone who just barfed her guts out into a toilet. Back out in the bar, my hand instinctively goes to the small crossbody purse that has my keys and ID in it. The hot biker follows me. Glancing around half-fearfully, I notice that Gonzalo and his friend are nowhere to be seen.

"Where did they go?" I ask, half to myself.

The biker chuckles. "I imagine Thorn and Beast gave them an incentive to get the fuck out of here if they knew what was good for them."

I should be relieved that I escaped Gonzalo's bad intentions. But a spike of dismay shoots through me all the same. It was a stroke of luck that I even managed to find him here at this bar. Now that he knows I was looking for him, I've lost the element of surprise. I'm no closer to finding my sister than I was before I got here. Maybe even further away.

"Thanks again," I murmur lamely to the biker, choking back tears that are threatening to surface.

If he notices I'm close to crying again, he doesn't say anything. "Don't mention it." The ghost of a smile plays across his sensual lips. "It's been a while since I got to punch an asshole. Felt good."

"Well, bye," I nod distractedly, and turn toward the front door of the bar. The biker's hand shoots out and grips my bicep, stopping me in my tracks.

"Where you going?" he asks.

I frown in confusion. "Home." I sway just a little bit in place, feeling kind of foggy. "My car's out front."

"Oh, no you don't. You're not driving anywhere."

"Why not?" I blink a few times, his face suddenly out of focus.

"Because you may still have some drug in your system. You're gonna need to wait around here until we can tell for sure."

"I'll be okay," I scoff, waving my hand in his face and almost stumbling. He catches me, a worried look in his eyes.

"No you won't." He puts an arm around my shoulders, holding me up. Peering into my eyes, he seems to see something he doesn't like. "Shit. Yeah, you're in no shape to drive."

I open my mouth to protest, but close it again as it dawns on me he might be right. It feels like I'm starting to get really, really drunk, even though I've only had one beer. I can't quite get my eyes to focus, or my muscles to work right. As much as I hate to admit it, I know I'd be crazy to try to drive in this condition. In a confused haze, I wonder how long it will last, and what I'm going to do until then.

The biker frowns, like he's considering options. "Look, we better get you home so you can lie down," he says finally. "Beast, Thorn," he calls out to his two friends, who are back at their bar stools with drinks in front of them. "I'm taking off. See you later."

"Later, brother," the larger one calls back, lifting a finger at us.

The biker takes my hand and leads me outside into the cool evening air. I try to focus on walking and staying upright, but I'm distracted by how huge his hand is as it envelops mine. And how rough the skin is. I start to giggle to myself. *I'm holding hands with a biker.* It seems so absurd. Actually, everything's starting to seem kind of absurd.

He stops us at a huge, low-slung, powerful looking motorcycle. "You gonna be okay to ride on the back of my Harley?" he asks in a worried tone, letting go of my hand. "All you gotta do is hold onto me and not fall off."

I think about it, and flex my fingers open and closed to make sure my arms still work. They seem to.

"Sure," I mumble. "I can do that."

Watching me carefully, as though he's afraid I might fall over, he slings a leg over the seat and straddles the machine. "Okay, get on," he orders, nodding behind him.

My balance is off, so I have to put one hand on his shoulder to get my foot over the bike. Under the fabric of his T-shirt, his muscles tense. Belatedly, I realize this is probably not a man most people just touch without asking. "Sorry," I mumble. The dress I'm wearing rides up a little as I raise my leg and climb over. Quickly, I yank it down under my butt, wishing I'd had the foresight to wear pants here instead.

Once I'm settled on the soft leather seat, the biker wordlessly leans down and grasps my leg just above the ankle. He places one of my feet, then the other, on some small foot pegs I didn't notice before. "Keep your feet on those pegs," he warns. "You don't want to lose your balance or burn your foot on an exhaust pipe."

"Okay," I agree. By now, I'm struggling to focus on what he's saying. Part of it's the drugs. But part of it is the distracting closeness of this stranger, who's already touched me more than any person has touched me in months.

"Put your arms around my waist," he commands.

I've never been on a motorcycle before, and he's basically the only thing keeping me from flying off of this one, so I do as he says. One weird silver lining about being roofied is that I'm not as scared about doing this as I would be if I was sober. Though, I probably should be. I've heard these things are death traps. Obediently, I lean forward and press myself against the back of his leather motorcycle vest, wrapping my arms around his waist like he told me to do.

It's strange to be this close to a total stranger. The soft, worn leather of his jacket contrasts with the roughness of the Lords of Carnage skull and wings image sewn onto the back of it. His body is strong and powerful-feeling. Solid, like warm steel. The vest is open at the front, so the palms of my hands end up bracing against his hard abs through his shirt. Even through the fabric, his skin is radiating heat. As he reaches forward to turn on the bike's engine, his stomach muscles ripple under my hands.

Between my legs, the hint of an ache begins, teased by the sudden vibrations of the bike.

"Where do you live?" he calls over the noise of the Harley.

"Oh. Uh, I don't live here." My brain's getting fuzzier every minute. "I'm staying at the Parkside Motel. Off of Highway Five."

"I know where it is," he nods. "Okay. Hang on."

And I do, trying as hard as I can to ignore the confused buzzing in my head and the low throb between my legs.

3
GUNNER

"I shouldn't have left my car at the bar," the girl mumbles as she stumbles off the back of my bike in front of the motel.

"Don't worry about it," I reassure her, and catch her arm so she doesn't fall. "I know Rosie, the owner. She's not the type to have it towed overnight. You can pick it up in the morning."

This motel's only about a mile and a half away from the bar, so the girl can easily walk it tomorrow once she's sobered up. Keeping my hand clutched around her bicep, I get off the bike and put my other arm around her shoulder to stop her swaying. She weaves on her legs but manages to stay upright. Together, we make it to the door she says is hers: number seven.

Once we get to her room, I prop her up against the outside wall next to the door and fish in her little purse until I find the key. She's so out of it that she doesn't do anything to protest that I'm digging through her bag. The lock's kind of fussy and I have to jiggle the knob to get the key to work. Eventually, I manage to open the door and help her through it.

I've passed by the Parkside Motel probably hundreds of times on my bike, but I've never actually been inside the place. Even for a run-down looking hole like this, the room is dingy. Ugly brown carpet shows the wear of the high-traffic areas in the dim light from the small lamp by the door. Everything smells like stale cigarette smoke and old dirt. It's not the kind of place a girl like her should be staying. Not by a long shot. *There's gotta be better places around here than this dump,* I start to think, but stop myself. *None of your business, Gun. Get her inside, make sure she's safe, and get on your way.*

Inside the room, I notice that apart from a single small backpack sitting unopened on one of the beds, there's no sign that it's even occupied. *She must have just arrived today.* It looks like she checked in, tossed her bag on the bed, and then immediately went straight from here to the bar.

Which means she's either an alcoholic, or a girl on a mission. And she sure as hell doesn't look like an alcoholic.

The girl's practically sleeping against my shoulder, so I drag her over to the nearest bed and sit down on it with her. As soon as her ass hits the mattress, she gives an audible sigh of relief and collapses, flopping onto her back and closing her eyes.

"I'm so tired," she complains. "My head hurts."

"I know. That's the drug," I tell her.

Even lying there like that, legs kind of splayed out off of the bed, she's fucking beautiful. I can't help but take a few seconds just to look at her. Her face is pale, almost translucent. I'm guessing that's partly because she's exhausted. There's a faint flush to her high, delicate cheekbones. Her lips are parted slightly. They're soft-looking, and plump. In another situation, in another, less shitty motel room, I'd fucking love to see them wrapped around my cock. As if in agreement, my dick jumps to attention in my pants. *Down, motherfucker.* This ain't the time or the place.

It sure as hell could be the woman, though. I'd fuck her in a heartbeat.

My eyes glide down to her breasts, which are rising and falling slowly and evenly. She's probably about to fall asleep. Shit, she's fucking lucky I'm the one who came across her tonight and helped her out. Helpless as she is right now, a lot of the fucking pigs in that bar would have taken advantage of this situation. Personally, I don't get my rocks off fucking a chick who isn't all there to enjoy it.

Apparently, the piece of shit who drugged her doesn't feel the same way.

As I sit there, watching the girl fall asleep, I wonder again what the hell she was doing in that bar tonight. Now that I know it looks like she came to town specifically to go there, I can't help but try to imagine the scenario in my head. She probably went there to confront that asshole. If he hadn't tried to roofie her, I might have assumed she was a jealous ex-girlfriend. She sure as hell doesn't look like the kind of girl who'd get involved with a dirtbag like that, though. I've seen stranger things, for sure. But I can't imagine why he'd drug her if he could have just fucked her without it. So that doesn't seem like it's the story.

Why the fuck are you here, little girl?

I don't even know her name. I would have asked her once we got here, but I didn't have time before she fell asleep. And she's looking so peaceful I don't want to wake her up now. Gingerly, I stand up from the bed, being careful not to jostle her too much, but it looks like she's down for the count. I slide her body up on the mattress, so her head's on one of the pillows and her legs aren't hanging over the side. Pulling off her sandals one by one, I toss them on the floor over by the nightstand. Then I grab her purse and lift her up enough to pull the strap over and off of her. She frowns in her sleep and moans a little in protest, but quiets when I lay her back down on the mattress.

Inside the little bag, there's an older model cell phone, a small wad of bills, and a driver's license. I take the license out and walk over to the dim lamp to hold it under the light.

Alix Andrea Cousins.

From Virginia.

Huh. So she definitely isn't from around here.

I toss the license back in her bag and put it on the floor next to her sandals. Then I take a deep breath and look around the room.

My work is done. She's here, she's safe. She'll be hung over but mostly fine tomorrow.

I should go, and let her get her sleep. Maybe leave a note reminding her what happened, and where her car is. Just in case the drug fucks with her memory.

But for some reason, my feet don't seem to be moving me toward the door.

Fuck.

I know she'll probably be all right if I leave her here by herself. I'm pretty sure we got at least some of the Rohypnol or whatever it was out of her system. But I just can't quite do it. I want to make sure she's okay when the drug wears off.

Goddamnit. Looks like I'm spending the night in a shitty motel bed. And for all the wrong reasons.

I walk over to Alix's bed and pull a corner of the bedspread up and over her. She stirs and sighs contentedly.

Then, with an irritated shake of my head that I'm such a fucking dumbass, I grab the room key from the table by the door. It's still pretty early. Not nearly early enough to go to bed. I know there's a convenience store half a mile down the road in the opposite direction from the Smiling Skull. I'll grab myself a couple beers, and come back here to drink them until I'm tired enough to go to sleep.

4
ALIX

My head is pounding worse than the worst hangover I ever had when I finally drift up into consciousness.

At first, I'm so disoriented that I don't know where I am. Whatever I'm sleeping on is so hard that for a second, I don't even think it's a bed. It's sure as hell not *my* bed, anyway. Which means I'm not at home. My eyes still closed, I frown and try to remember what happened last night. It comes back to me slowly through the brain fog. I was driving from Virginia, to where I thought Eden was, to try to find her. I remember arriving at the motel, then dumping my stuff and going to the bar…

Then arguing with Gonzalo. And then there was the biker guy who beat him up. And the biker telling me he saw Gonzalo slip a roofie into my beer. Then things get hazier, but I think I remember starting to feel woozy, and the biker guy taking me out of the bar and putting me on his motorcycle…

My eyes fly open.

"Hey. You're up," says a voice over by the door. "Let's go get some breakfast."

I sit up and give a little yelp of surprise. Wild-eyed, I look half-terrified in the direction of the voice.

It's the biker guy from last night. He's sitting in the single chair next to the table.

"What are you doing in here?" I gasp.

"I decided to stick around to make sure you were okay," he replies evenly. One corner of his mouth goes up in the hint of a smile. "How you feelin'?"

I start to panic, wondering what he's done to me while I've been asleep. But I'm still wearing the dress I had on yesterday, and my body doesn't feel any different, except for my pounding head. I risk a quick glance over at the second bed. The bedspread looks rumpled, as though someone spent the night lying on top of it.

Warily, I look back at him. "I've felt better."

He laughs, revealing white, even teeth in a vaguely wolfish grin. "I bet. But I'm hungry as hell, and you should be, too. We should get some food in you. It'll help clear your head." He stands up from the chair and nods toward the door. "Come on. I'll take you to breakfast. My treat."

I want to refuse. I almost do. But I'm down to my last

hundred dollars or so, and the prospect of getting a hot meal without even having to pay for it breaks down any resolve I have.

"Okay," I accept softly. "Thanks. I appreciate it. But let me run to the bathroom first."

"I'll be outside," he says, standing.

I briefly consider running to the door and locking it from the inside once it closes behind him. But the plain fact of the matter is, this man is at least twice or three times as strong as I am. He could easily break down any door between us. And if he'd wanted to do something to me, he's had ample opportunity already. So instead, even though I wonder if I'm doing something completely crazy, I go into the tiny, cramped bathroom and carefully close the door behind me. I pee, then splash some cold water on my face and rinse my mouth out. Back out in the main room, I find my sandals, slip them on, and grab my purse. The key to the room is on the little table, and I toss it into my bag and wander out the door behind him.

Outside, it's a bright, sunny day already. It doesn't feel like early morning any more. I must have slept longer than I thought, thanks to the roofie Gonzalo put in my drink. The biker guy is already astride his motorcycle, waiting for me. *I should have changed into jeans,* I think ruefully, and almost go back inside. But then the bike starts up and the man gestures for me to get on. *Well, somehow I managed to ride here in this dress last night, so I guess I can pull it off again.* I toss the long strap of my bag over my head so it's secure, then awkwardly get on and straddle the seat behind the man.

"I don't even know your name," I call over the roar of the engine.

"Gunner," he calls back.

"Nice to meet you, Gunner," I reply, feeling like a total moron. "I'm Alix."

In response, he merely grunts. Gingerly, I wrap my arms around his waist, and he pulls out onto the highway.

Ten minutes later, we're seated in a booth at a crowded diner. Delicious smells of hash browns and coffee are wafting toward us. Up until now, I wasn't really hungry, but the food aromas remind me that I haven't eaten since lunch yesterday. My stomach growls impatiently as I ponder the menu the waitress gave me. I feel like I could eat a horse, but I settle on the country breakfast with pancakes, eggs, and sausage. And coffee, of course.

"Good deal," Gunner nods approvingly. "I was afraid you were gonna order some bullshit egg white, no-food omelet or something."

"Not a chance. You were right, I'm starving." I take a sip of the hot coffee the waitress just brought me. "Oh, that's good," I sigh. I take another sip, savoring the taste and the warmth.

"So," Gunner begins after a moment, leaning back on his side of the booth. "You want to tell me what you were doing in that bar last night?"

Shit. I guess I should have known he might try to pry into that. "Look, I'm sorry," I say, "But it's really none of your business."

He cocks a brow at me and smirks through his beard. "None of my business?"

"No offense, but you're a total stranger, Gunner."

"I'm a total stranger who saved your ass last night."

He's right, of course. Maybe I do owe him some sort of explanation, as payback for putting himself out there for me.

"I'm sorry," I murmur, chastened. "You didn't have to do any of what you did. It's just… well, it's kind of personal."

"He your boyfriend?"

"What? No!" I start laughing, the idea's so ludicrous. "No, no. Nothing like that. I'm just… looking for someone. I think Gonzalo might know where she is."

"Someone?"

"My sister," I admit.

He nods, considering this. "*She* his girlfriend?"

I look down at the table. "Something like that," I say

softly. "Look, can we talk about something else, at least until the food gets here? I'm still feeling a little queasy, and my head hurts."

He gives me an easy grin and lifts his chin once. "Sure. What do you want to talk about?"

"Um. I don't know."

"Hey, you don't want to talk about your sister. You pick the conversation subject."

I sigh. "Fine," I say, a little irritated. "Do you go to the Smiling Skull very often?"

He smirks again. "From time to time." He doesn't go any further, and after a few seconds I realize he's purposely not saying much so I'll have to keep asking questions to keep the conversation going. Jackass.

I shake my head and snort softly. "Okay. What's the Lords of Carnage?" I ask, glancing at one of the patches on his leather vest.

"It's an MC out of Tanner Springs, about an hour west of here."

"MC?"

"Motorcycle club."

"And what's a 'road captain'?" I say, reading from another patch.

"It's more or less what it says. When the MC's on the road, I'm the captain. I organize our runs, and make sure shit goes as planned."

"A run?" I wrinkle my nose. "Like a group motorcycle ride?"

"Yeah. Like that."

The waitress arrives with our food, and for a few minutes, neither of us says anything as we eat. I'm so hungry and the food's so good that I have to restrain myself from moaning as I chew. It's an effort to eat slowly, and that takes up all my mental energy for a while.

Eventually, I take a last bite of sausage and lean back against the faux leather of the back rest. My head has finally stopped pounding so hard, and my mind is starting to feel clearer. "Oh, my God, I'm stuffed," I sigh happily. "I feel *so* much better."

"Glad to hear it." Gunner shoots me a sexy grin. I don't know if it's because I'm finally starting to feel human again, but that grin sets something off inside me that feels almost like electricity. It's like just for one dizzying, mesmerizing second, he's not some dangerous stranger who inexplicably helped me last night. And I'm not some stupid girl who's completely out of her element on some hopeless mission to find her sister. For just one tiny moment, there's this little signal that feels like it's just between us. Like the grin is *just* for me, and no one else. Like it's the prelude to something… *intimate*. His eyes are locked on mine, and all of a sudden all I can think about is how impossibly blue they are.

Then I realize I'm staring at him, and quickly drop my gaze.

A long second passes.

"So. Now that you're feeling better," he continues as if nothing just happened, "you said you're looking for your sister."

My head feels like it's starting to spin again. But this time, it has nothing to do with the drug Gonzalo gave me. My mind just flashed back to an image from last night, when I was on the back of Gunner's bike, my arms wrapped around him as he drove me to the motel. I remember the masculine smell of his leather and the hard muscles of his torso under his shirt. But mostly, I remember how *sexual* it felt, sitting back there pressed up against him.

My skin starts to feel all tingly at the memory, and even though Gunner's all the way across the table, all of a sudden he feels uncomfortably close.

"Yeah," I murmur, trying to focus on what he's saying.

"So, if you're staying in a motel, you're obviously not from around here," he prompts.

"No. Uh, Virginia."

He gives a brief nod, almost like my answer passes some sort of test or something. "So, why the fuck are you staying in that dump? There's gotta be better places around here than the Parkside Motel."

"It's all I can afford," I admit. *Actually, I can't even afford that.*

His innocent question starts me down the path of lamenting again how much money I spent for a night in that hovel of a room. Then, suddenly, my heart jumps in panic.

"Oh, my gosh, what time is it?" I blurt out.

Gunner glances over my shoulder to a spot above the counter, where there must be a clock hanging on the wall. "Ten-thirty."

"Shit!" I cry. "Checkout time's at eleven. They'll charge me for another night if I don't leave the room in time! The manager told me they're very strict about it. I need to go!"

Gunner raises his eyebrows at me. I feel my face start to turn red. I don't need anyone knowing the direness of my financial situation. Certainly not this near-total stranger who's already saved my neck once. But the reality is a stark one: if I have to pay for another night, I won't even have enough money to make it back to Virginia. I'll sleep in my car if I have to. But I can't afford any more motels if I want to find Eden before my money runs out completely.

"Please," I beg, ignoring the heat in my cheeks. "You've been so kind to me already. I really don't want to take any more advantage of you. But could you take me back to the motel to get my bag and check out?"

Gunner contemplates me for a second, his face expressionless. Then he gives me a brief nod and raises his hand for the check. "Okay. I'll get you back there in time."

"Thank you so much!" While he pays the bill, I run to the bathroom and take a couple of seconds to compose myself. In the mirror, I look pale and frightened. I forgot to brush my hair this morning, and my white dress is definitely the worse for wear. I hope I get back to the motel in time to change into something else before I have to be out of the room.

We end up making it back with ten minutes to spare. Gunner waits outside and smokes a cigarette while I throw on a pair of jeans and a T-shirt, pull my hair into a pony, and give my teeth a quick brush. Stuffing the few items I've unpacked back into my small backpack, I grab the key and am out the door walking toward the front office at five minutes to eleven, relief flooding my veins.

5
GUNNER

I'm standing outside the motel room, finishing a smoke, when my phone buzzes in my pocket. I pull it out just as Alix emerges, backpack slung over her shoulder. She's changed into faded jeans and a fitted dark red T-shirt. Her hair's pulled back from her face into a messy ponytail. She looks fresh, and casual, and sexy as shit.

"I just have to return this," she says, holding up the key and jiggling it.

I lift my chin. "Got it. I'll be right here."

She flashes me a brief smile and turns toward the front office. I pause for a moment to appreciate her spectacular ass in a different package. When she's disappeared around the corner, I regretfully drag my eyes away and look down at my phone. It's a text from Thorn.

> Church this aftn. Rock has some business with the DDs to run by us

I nod at the phone as though it's Thorn himself and hit reply:

> I'll be there

I shove the thing back in my pocket and take a last drag of my smoke. I wonder what the Death Devils have in mind. They're a club to the east of us — in fact, I'm in Death Devils territory right now. The Devils and our club have been inching toward an alliance, which started in part because of a desire on the part of both our clubs to strengthen our numbers. And to unite against a growing threat from the Iron Spiders, before the Lords took out their president.

Now, even though the Spiders threat looks to be neutralized, it's still in our best interests to strengthen the partnership with the Death Devils if possible. We sold them the last of our weapons shipments a while back, when our club decided to get out of gun running. Now they've largely taken over the business we walked away from. The Devils' president, Oz, is kind of a closed book, but his men seem to respect the shit out of him, and he hasn't fucked us over yet.

I'm musing about what Oz's club might be wanting to propose to the Lords, when shouting from the motel's main office shakes me out of my thoughts. It's Alix's voice. I put out my smoke and go over to see what the fuck's going on.

When I get inside, she's arguing with a fat, greasy-looking guy who's standing behind the counter. Alix is waving her arms and pointing at a clock on the wall, which reads eleven ten.

"You know damn well that clock is fast!" she yells. "You do this on purpose!"

"It's the customer's responsibility to be out of the room in a timely manner," the guy smirks. "This clock is the one we go by."

"I am *not* paying for another night," Alix fumes.

"If you're unable or unwilling to pay, we'll just have to get the local authorities involved," the guy says in a smug tone, reaching his fat fucking hand toward the phone on his desk.

"I don't think that's gonna be necessary," I interrupt, walking up to the counter. The fat fucker turns toward me, a flash of apprehension on his face.

"Sir, are you with this woman?"

"I am." I put my elbows on the counter and lean in toward him, until my face is maybe a foot from his. I've easily got five inches on him, and even though we're probably about the same weight, his is mostly from fat.

"I'm sorry," he half-stammers, his eyes moving from Alix

to me. "But it's our policy to charge for another night if a customer fails to vacate their room in a timely manner. I explained this to her yesterday when I checked her in, and she said she understood."

"I can understand that," I say easily. "Trouble is, your clock's broken."

"No, it's not," he says, and rolls his eyes.

I fucking hate it when people roll their eyes.

This fat fuck doesn't seem to be getting the message. I straighten, walk over to the wall, and take the clock down from the nail it's hanging on. Bringing it back to the desk, I turn it over and bring it down hard on the counter, smashing its face. Both Alix and the greasy guy jump back, the guy visibly blanching.

"Huh," I mutter in a puzzled tone. I reach in through the splinters of broken plastic and move the minute hand back, until the clock reads ten fifty-five. "I guess you're right. I thought it was broken, but it must have fixed itself." I toss the thing, frisbee-like, across the counter. It crashes loudly against the back wall of the office. Then I grab the room key lying on the counter in front of Alix and toss it after the clock.

"You have a nice day, now," I say.

The fat pig is so shocked he doesn't say a word as I grab Alix's hand and pull her back outside.

"Holy shit," Alex hisses as the office door swings shut behind us. "I can't believe you did that."

"Problem?"

"No!" she starts to giggle, and then snorts loudly, bringing her hand to her face. "Oh, my God, that was epic!" Then she's full-out laughing, hard enough that she has to stop walking and lean her hand against the outside wall of the motel to steady herself. She doubles up and gasps for breath, laughing until there are tears in her eyes.

Watching her let go like this, it makes me realize how pinched and serious she's been up to this point. Knowing I'm the reason for it — it does something to my chest. Like it's constricting and expanding at the same time.

She continues to shake in helpless laughter leaning against the side of the building for support. Before I know it, I'm laughing with her.

"Come on," I eventually chuckle. "Let's get the fuck out of this shithole."

Alix is still giggling when we get to my bike. "Thank you so much for that, Gunner," she says, her eyes sparkling. "That was the funniest thing I've seen in… God, I have no idea."

"My pleasure. That fucker deserved it." He's luckier than he knows that I didn't beat his damn face in, just for the pleasure of breaking a few of his teeth. "Come on. I'll take you back to your car."

I help Alix put on her backpack, then get on the bike. She slides on behind me, less awkwardly now that she's not wearing a dress. Automatically, her arms go around my waist, the seat sliding her forward a little so she's snug up against my back. I can feel her still giggling a little bit as I start the bike, her tits moving against my back as she does. My cock tightens in my jeans, and I remember how tough it was last night to look at her sprawled on the bed and not be able to do anything about it.

Shit. The sooner I get her back to her car and send her on her way, the better. I've been trying to keep her safe from assholes since I met her, but if she's not careful she'll need saving from *me* next.

The trip back to the Smiling Skull only takes a couple minutes, since now I can go full-speed without worrying about Alix falling off the bike. The bar doesn't open until this afternoon, and the parking lot is deserted except for what must be her car. It's a rusty as hell, dark blue Civic with a body style from the early nineties. This thing must have close to two-hundred thousand miles on it. I think back to how hard she fought against paying for another night at the motel, and realize Alix must be pretty goddamn broke if this is what she drives.

I slow the bike and stop in the spot next to the Civic. Turning the engine off, I wait for her to get off, then stand to face her.

"Well," Alix says, flashing me a suddenly shy smile. "Thank you so much for everything, Gunner. I never properly thanked you for buying me breakfast. And, well, for everything else." She lifts her shoulders and spreads her hands.

"What are you gonna do now?" I ask her.

"Um…" She glances back toward her car. "I dunno. I'm going to keep looking for my sister."

"You're not coming back to this bar, are you?" I ask sharply. "Are you gonna go looking for that Gonzalo guy again?"

"I don't know," she admits. Her face crumples into a mask of worry, and it makes my chest hurt to see her smile go away. "I don't think Gonzalo is going to tell me anything. But I'm *sure* he knows where she is. Or at least he *did* know."

"Alix, are you gonna tell me what the hell's going on here?" I demand.

My voice comes out so gruff and angry it surprises me. It seems to surprise her, too.

"I…" she begins, looking at me with wide, confused eyes. "Gunner, this isn't your fight. No, I wasn't planning on telling you any more."

I lean against her driver's side door so she can't open it, and cross my arms. "Well, that's gonna change. Talk."

"Why?" she asks, a sudden flash of defiance in her eyes.

"Because I said so."

I'm not leaving until she does tell me. And she can't leave until I let her into her car. We're at an impasse, and we will be until she realizes there's only one way forward.

For a second I think she's going to keep arguing with me. Then her shoulders slump a little bit, and she pulls her backpack off and tiredly sets it on the ground beside her. "There's not that much to tell," she sighs. "My sister left town, and I don't know where she is. I'm worried about her. She was seeing Gonzalo, and I'm almost positive she left with him. Or because of him, anyway."

"How did you know to come here?"

Her eyes flick to the side, toward the closed bar. "She had an app on her smart phone so I could track her. For safety. She had one on her phone for me, too. The last place the phone said she was was here." She takes in a deep breath and lets it out, defeated. "And then she must have taken the app off, or deleted me, because she disappeared."

"So you came here hoping to find her?"

"Yeah. But instead, I just found Gonzalo." Her face twists into an expression of disgust. "He told me they broke up and that he doesn't know where she is."

"Who is this Gonzalo guy anyway?" He's not a biker, Or anyway he's not in an MC. He wasn't wearing a cut, and wasn't flying any colors.

"I don't know, exactly." One hand goes up and pulls distractedly at the end of her blond ponytail. "He just showed up one day with my sister. In Lynchburg. That's where I'm from." She shakes her head in frustration. "I know he was involved in some shady stuff. My sister started seeing him. Off and on, at first. My mom was furious, of course. But I think that just made Eden more determined to be with him." Alix looks up with me ruefully. "My mom and Eden didn't get along."

"Didn't?"

"My mom's dead. About six months ago." Her voice is flat, but a little tremble of her chin tells me she's trying to keep her emotions under control. "I thought maybe her dying would finally wake Eden up. That once she didn't have Mom around to shock anymore, she'd stop trying to play the bad girl and walk away from Gonzalo. But instead, it just made her into more of a wild child."

Something about the look of pain on her face makes me want to reach out to touch her. Comfort her. But I make myself keep my distance, because I'm pretty sure I know where it will lead if I do. There's been a spark of something between Alix and me at since least the restaurant. I can feel it, and I know she can, too.

"Does she know you're looking for her?" I ask instead, trying to ignore the untimely stirring of my cock.

"I don't know," she shrugs. "She probably suspects it, if she deleted the tracking app on her phone." Alix looks down at the ground. "The last time I saw her, we had a fight. She told me to leave her the hell alone, and stop trying to take care of her. That she could live her own life." Her eyes fill with tears, but she opens them wide to keep them from spilling and clears her throat. "I know she'd probably be pissed if she knew I was still trying to find her. Maybe I should just leave her alone. I just…" Her voice breaks and she clears her throat again. "I just want to know she's okay. That's all. After that, if she wants me to go away, I will."

Fuck. This is some heavy duty shit. Looking at Alix last night in the bar, I just assumed she was some homecoming queen with a bad boy fetish, slumming it with the lowlifes for some kind of thrill. I can't help but have some serious respect for her now, knowing that she barged into a biker bar with no fear and no backup just to find her sister.

Of course, it was stupid as hell, too. But even so, it was gutsy.

I'm about to say some stupid cliche'd shit about how sorry I am, when an idea hits me.

It's probably crazy — hell, it's *definitely* crazy. But once it's in my head I can't push it out.

Fuck it. Why not.

"Look. Alix." I begin, barely able to believe I'm going to suggest this. "I have to get back to my place for some business this afternoon. I live about an hour west of here, in Tanner Springs." She nods and starts to turn to her car, but I stop her. "Wait. Come with me. I've got a house, and a spare bedroom. You can stay there. At least long enough to figure out if your sister's still in the area."

Instead of being grateful, Alix looks alarmed. "No thanks, Gunner," she starts to stammer. "I, uh, have to be getting back. To Lynchburg."

Her eyes flick away from mine as she says the name of her town. She's lying, I can tell. She's not going back. She just told me she's going to keep looking for her sister. But whether she's trying not to impose on me, or she's afraid I'm going to try to take her home and force myself on her, I don't know.

"Horseshit," I rasp. "You're not going back to Lynchburg. You and I both know that."

She glances up at me guiltily.

"Look, darlin'," I continue. "If I was gonna jump you, I already would have done it by now in that shitty motel room. Unlike that piece of shit Gonzalo, I don't need to trick or drug women into sleeping with me." I look her in the eye, trying to ignore the fact that I'd love to bend her over the hood of her car and do nasty things to her, just to hear her moan my name.

She's frowning at me, clearly still planning to keep refusing my offer. "I'm just trying to help you out, Alix. I swear," I say. It's mostly the truth. "It seems like you could use some help right about now. And if you were willing to fight that hard back at the motel to not pay for another night, I'm guessing you could use a free place to stay for a while."

She doesn't say anything in response, but I can tell she's wavering.

"Tell me I'm wrong."

"No," she whispers. "You're not."

"Look," I continue. "I'll even go stay at the MC's clubhouse, and give you the house to yourself, if it makes you feel safer."

Alix is silent for a few seconds. Then for a few more.

"Why are you helping me?" she finally asks in a small voice.

"Fuck if I know," I growl. "But come on, before I change my mind."

6
ALIX

I follow Gunner's bike in my car all the way to Tanner Springs. The whole distance there, I argue with myself about whether I should really be accepting his offer to stay at his place. A couple of times I almost turn the car around. In the end, though, the offer's too good to pass up. The prospect of sleeping in my car for the foreseeable future doesn't thrill me. And no matter what, I'm committed to searching for Eden until I find her. Especially after what happened with Gonzalo last night.

It's a little daunting, though, the idea of staying in the house of someone I barely know. Especially someone like Gunner. I'm already so far in his debt. And I'm uncomfortably attracted to him, to boot. It's a feeling that makes me more than a little wary. I keep expecting him to drop the pretense of being a decent guy, and demand payback. And with men like him, the kind of payback they usually want is something they'll just *take*. Whether you want to give it to them or not.

Then I realize I'm lumping him into the same group with people like Gonzalo, and silently berate myself for judging him like that. Sure, I met Gunner in a seedy bar filled with bikers and lowlifes. But even though Gunner's a biker himself, he's already proved he's not like Gonzalo. Not at all. At least, not when he doesn't want to be. After all, he said himself that if he'd wanted to take advantage of me, he already had ample opportunity when I was passed out in the motel room. And that's definitely true. So even though I don't understand his motives, I can't help but grudgingly believe him.

He probably doesn't find you attractive. It's not like you're likely to be his type, after all. You're hardly like the busty biker chicks in that bar. By comparison, you look like a ten year-old boy.

I should find that idea comforting. It really should be a relief.

But instead, it gives me an odd, sinking feeling in my stomach.

My God, am I *disappointed* he doesn't want to have his way with me?

I'm so surprised and exasperated with myself that I actually laugh out loud in the car. "God, Alix, you are *ridiculous*," I tell myself with a snort of disbelief. My words hang there in the air, taunting me, as I continue to ride behind Gunner, toward a town called Tanner Springs.

* * *

I only know we've arrived at our destination because of the rectangular green sign just outside the city limits. No buildings are visible yet. Shortly after we pass the sign, Gunner lifts a hand and makes a motion in the air to let me know we'll be turning right soon. I slow my car to just over the new speed limit, and flip on my turn signal shortly after he does. A few seconds later, I see where he's planning to turn. We pull off the highway onto a residential road, which ends up leading to a neighborhood of small and medium-sized houses at the edge of town. I zigzag behind Gunner's bike for a few more minutes, winding through the streets. Finally, he hand signals a left turn and pulls into the driveway of a white bungalow with dark gray trim and a small porch in front.

Not wanting to impose, I start to park my car on the street, but Gunner waves me up to pull in next to his bike. "You're staying here as my guest," he rumbles at me through my open window when I've shut off my engine. "You can park in the driveway."

"Thank you," I mumble, and hoist myself out of the car. I reach in and grab my backpack from the passenger seat. When I've pulled it out and straightened, I catch Gunner casting an appreciative look at my ass.

"Sorry, just enjoying the scenery," he grins sexily. "Come

on, let's get you situated."

I shoot him an accusing look and follow him to the front door, feeling indignant but also… kind of weirdly happy.

Dammit. I can't believe there's a part of me that *wants* him to find me attractive. *This is not what you're here for, Alix*, I tell myself crossly. *Besides which, the last thing you need is to get yourself in the same kind of stupid mess Eden did.* My sister is absolutely gorgeous, but she never seems to really believe it unless some guy is chasing after her. Her need to have male eyes on her to feel important has been the source of many of Eden's bad decisions. And there have been a *lot* of them.

I'll be damned if I'm going to let myself go down that same path. Especially when the whole reason I'm here is to make sure her bad decisions haven't gotten her in real trouble this time.

Gunner unlocks the door and holds the screen open for me to go in. The house is small, but inviting inside. The living room is painted in reds and tans, and arranged with comfortable-looking furniture. A brick fireplace anchors one side of the room. The living room leads into a dining room with a dark wood table that's got some bills and other papers on it.

"I wasn't exactly expecting guests," Gunner says easily as he leads me down a short hallway. "Bathroom's over here to the right. Towels and shit are in the closet behind the door." He continues to the end of the hall, where there are two doors, one to the left and one to the right. The left one must be his bedroom, because he pushes open the right-hand side door and motions me through. "Here's your room," he says.

It's small and sparsely furnished, with a double bed, a standing lamp, and a short, square dresser. "The closet has my shit in it," Gunner tells me, "But the dresser's all yours."

"Thank you again," I murmur.

"Stop thanking me, Alix. It's getting boring."

"I'm sorry." My face grows hot.

"It's fine. But seriously, knock it off, okay?" Gunner pulls out his phone and grimaces a little. "Look, I gotta go. Some club business to take care of. Make yourself at home. There's another house key hanging on one of the hooks next to the back door. You can take that so you can come and go as you please."

"Okay," I nod. He shoves his phone back in his pocket and looks at me. Our eyes lock for a second.

And I realize, once again, that we're completely alone.

God, his eyes are blue.

My skin starts to feel kind of goosebumpy.

I remember how rough and callused his hands are. I wonder what they'd feel like roaming over my body.

Stop. It.

"Okay, then. Stay out of trouble." His voice is gruff, but then Gunner *winks* at me, one corner of his mouth lifting. My stomach does a little flip. "When I get back, we can talk about how to find your sis."

The clomp of Gunner's boots gets softer and softer as he walks back down the hallway. Then the front door opens and shuts behind him.

The roar of his Harley engine has completely disappeared when I realize I'm still standing in the middle of the bedroom, in a sort of daze.

I blink and shake my head, and snort softly at how ridiculous I'm being. I've never really had a man affect me like this before. It's like my body is on constant high alert when he's around. My nipples are standing at attention, waiting to be touched.

Waiting for him *to touch them.*

My skin is practically *buzzing*. And Gunner's not even here anymore.

He, on the other hand, seems more or less completely unaffected by my presence.

Except he seems to think my ass is okay.

I begin repeating my new mantra, *It's* good *that Gunner doesn't want me. It's* good *that Gunner doesn't want me,* as I sit down on the bed. Opening up my backpack, I take out the few belongings I brought with me. The bedspread under me is a soft, homey quilt, obviously handmade. I wonder who made it for him. I can't see Gunner buying something like this. For one thing, handmade quilts are crazy expensive. And besides, it doesn't really seem like his style. I imagine a grandmother giving it to him, or an aunt, and then I have to laugh because I can barely even envision someone like him having a granny. He's so… masculine. And *hard*. It's almost impossible to imagine he was ever a little boy, or a baby. Gunner seems like he just sprang into the world like he is right now. Hot, sexy as hell, muscled and tattooed.

My skin does that tingly thing again.

It's good *that Gunner doesn't want me. It's* good *that Gunner doesn't want me…*

I pull out the couple of T-shirts and the few changes of underwear I brought with me, and stash them with a couple of other items in the top drawer of the empty dresser. Then I take out the rumpled white shirt dress I was wearing yesterday. It needs to be washed, but I don't want to snoop around for a washer and dryer in Gunner's house. Instead, I go to the bathroom and hand wash it, using some of the small bottle of shampoo I grabbed from the motel. I wring it out and hang it over a towel bar to dry, placing a hand towel I found in the little closet under it so it won't drip on the floor.

That task done, I wander out into the hallway, feeling suddenly restless. Gunner hasn't even been gone half an hour. I wonder when he'll come back. If he's still gone by dinner time, should I just assume I'm on my own and eat without him? He told me to make myself at home, but I wouldn't feel right about eating his food.

I go into the kitchen, which is simple and kind of bare. Opening the fridge, I see there's hardly any food in it anyway, apart from a pizza box, a carton of milk, and some jars of pickles and condiments. It's actually sort of a relief to know I'll have to go out shopping for food. It gives me something to do until he gets back.

I wander out into the living room, noticing again how comfortable and lived-in it is, without being cluttered. It's obvious that a man lives here from the simple furnishings and the dark colors. The only things hanging on the wall are a couple of pictures of classic-looking bikes and a large flat-screen TV mounted above the fireplace. There are no photos of family or friends, I note with disappointment. Nothing personal that will tell me anything more about who Gunner is, or the people who are important to him.

In the dining room, I glance at the piles of papers, and glimpse an unopened envelope on one stack. I bend over to see the name and address typed on it. *Gunner Storgaard*, I read. A tiny little thrill of excitement runs up my spine that I've learned his last name. But then I feel bad for snooping, even if the envelope was right there on top.

To avoid any temptation to look at anything else on the table, I move off back down the hall to the guest room. I decide I'm going to go grocery shopping. Even though I'm almost out of money, I have to eat, after all. And if Gunner does come back in time for dinner tonight, I'd like to be able to make him something to thank him for his generosity. It won't be anything special, since I can't afford much. But luckily, from what I saw in the kitchen, it doesn't look like he'll be expecting a gourmet meal anyway.

I lean down and grab my little purse off the bed, then turn to walk back out into the hallway. As I do, I notice that I can see straight through into Gunner's bedroom from mine. Curiosity gets the better of me again. I tiptoe across the hall, even though there's no one else here, and peek inside.

The curtains are drawn, so the room is fairly dark. I can make out a king-size bed with dark-colored sheets. The covers are flung aside, as though he just got up. Even though I know better, I close my eyes for a second and imagine the mattress and pillow are still warm from his body. I remember the clean, masculine scent of him from this morning, when I was riding behind him on his bike.

A noise from outside startles me out of my thoughts. I turn and skitter back to my room, but after a few seconds I realize the sound isn't Gunner returning. Letting out a breath I didn't even realize I was holding, I scold myself once again for being too curious where he's concerned.

Groceries, I tell myself sternly. *And then figure out how you're going to find Eden. The sooner the better — so you can say goodbye to Gunner Storgaard for good.*

7
GUNNER

I don't know what time church is supposed to start. Thorn never told me in his text. But since today is Sunday, it's a pretty fair bet it won't be before mid-afternoon. Even though Thorn, Beast, and I weren't at the clubhouse last night, Saturday nights here are always pretty raucous. I'm guessing at least half the brothers will be nursing hangovers. And short of a true emergency, Rock would only call a meeting for once everyone's had some time to sleep it off.

Sure enough, when I walk in the door of the clubhouse, a bunch of the brothers are already here, but it's clear nothing's started yet. I lift my chin toward Thorn and Beast, who are over in one corner with Hawk and Brick. Thorn's laughing his ass off, and Beast's looking pissed. I'm guessing Thorn's getting a kick out of rehashing yesterday's arm wrestling story, since Hawk and Brick weren't around for it.

I start to make my way over them to join in the ribbing, when a tug on my arm stops me. "Hey, there, baby," coos a familiar voice. "Missed you last night."

Fuck. Heather. "Hey, darlin'," I drawl, turning to see the leggy redhead.

"I thought you'd be here at the clubhouse last night," she pouts prettily at me. "None of the other girls knew where you were."

Inwardly I groan. Heather's one of the new club girls. She's only been around a couple of months. We've fucked a few times, and she's a damn animal in the sack, but she doesn't seem to have gotten the memo that club girls are just that: they're property of the club. The way she hangs on me, you'd think we were goin' goddamn steady and she was wearing my fuckin' class ring, or something. Jesus.

"Had some other business to attend to," I mutter, detaching her long red nails from my bicep. Heather whines in protest and tries to cling on, but I give her a look that tells her I'm not playing around.

She drops her head and juts out her lower lip, looking at me from under her long, dark lashes. "You're no fun," she says breathily. "I waited all night for you."

"That'll teach you not to wait, then," I mutter, and continue over to my brothers. Even though Heather can deep throat like nobody's business, I'm starting to regret ever fucking her. The sooner she gets the message and starts chasing after one of the other men, the better. She'd be better off with a prospect — they're more likely to get moony over one of the regulars. But she won't give any of the non-patched men the time of day. She wants to be an old lady, that much is obvious. That ain't never gonna happen, though. Not with me, anyway.

Irritated, I shake Heather from my thoughts and go over and join the group. "Hey, brothers," I greet them.

"Gun!" Thorn cries, and slaps me on the back. "How the hell are ya? We thought yeh'd come back to the Skull last night."

"I'm good," I nod. "Did those fucks we gave a beatdown to ever show back up again?"

He snorts. "Not a chance, brother. I'm guessin' they spent the rest of their night tryin' to clean out the loads in their shorts. So, about that, whatever happened with that girl from the bar last night?" He flashes me a knowing grin. "She have anything to do with why you never came back?"

"She was pretty fucked up after that Gonzalo motherfucker put that roofie in her drink," I tell him. "I managed to get her back to the motel where she was staying without her falling off my bike."

"And?" Thorn prompts.

"And nothing, you fucking pig," I snarl. "She was drugged up. You think I'd take advantage of a woman who was basically unconscious? I'm not *that* fuckin' desperate."

"Jaysus, listen to the Boy Scout," he roars with laughter.

"So, you just took her home out of the goodness of your heart? What'll yeh be doin' next, helpin' little old ladies cross the street?"

Thorn's certain that isn't the end of the story. It's clear from the skeptical way he's looking at me. And he's right — even though he'd probably laugh his ass off and call me a pussy if I told him what really happened afterwards. Especially if I told him Alix is at my house right now, and that I still haven't fucked her. In the end, I figure there's no point telling him anything one way or another.

Just then, Ghost, our Sergeant at Arms, calls out to tell us it's time for church. All the men move into the chapel and take our usual spots around the table. Once we sit down and take care of the usual formalities, our president, Rock, tells us he's been approached by the Death Devils' prez to help their club with some upcoming runs.

"Oz got hold of me because the Devils are down a few men," he says. "A bunch of their members got caught up in a war between another club and one of their charters the next state over, and shit went bad. Five of the Devils landed in jail, and it looks like they'll all be doing a stint in county."

Ghost whistles. "That's some fucked up luck, right there."

"Yeah." Rock leans back. "So now they don't have enough men to do their runs. At least not for the time being. And they want our help."

"What kind of runs?" asks Lug Nut.

"The runs to our old associates," Angel, our vice-president, answers.

For the better part of a year, the Lords of Carnage has been completely legit, for better or worse. We got rid of the last of our illegal businesses — gun running — when things got too hot to handle. The newly elected mayor of our sleepy little down, Jarred Holloway, had started gunning for us — no pun intended. The Lords saw the writing on the wall. It was only a matter of time before even the inept, uniformed bags of skin at the Tanner Springs PD would manage to find — or plant — enough evidence to take the club down. In the meantime, they'd be following our every goddamn move.

So instead of giving them anything real to find on us, we sold off the last of our gun shipments to the Death Devils, and introduced them to our associates. For a mutually agreed-upon price, we let them take over our little piece of the Iron Pipeline. The Devils were only too happy to have our contacts — and to take over a business that was already well-established. With the blessing of the Lords of Carnage as their calling card to their new clients.

Now, apparently they're asking us to get back in.

"What kind of compensation are they offering us, in exchange for our services?" Thorn asks wryly.

"Negotiable." Rock shifts in his chair to look at him. "But even though Oz is a hard one to read, I think we might be able to pretty much name our price."

"It's probably a good idea regardless," muses Ghost, always the practical thinker. "Since the Iron Spiders went underground, we don't know when or if they'll surface again. It can't hurt us to have the Devils as firmly on our side as possible. Quid pro quo."

"Speaking of which. Tweak, you've been monitoring the Spiders' old clubhouse," Angel says, turning to our resident techie. "Any evidence of movement over there?"

"None," Tweak confirms. "I've still got cameras on the building and on the only road that goes there. There's been no activity in or out in from their old compound in months."

"We should go investigate in person," old Smiley chuckles. "See whether those fuckin' Spiders are still in their hole. See what they left behind."

Rock frowns and sets his jaw, considering. "We'll talk about that later," he mutters, and shifts in his seat. "In the meantime, we're talkin' about the Death Devils' proposal. Are we good to provide them some backup on our old gun running route?"

"I'm good with it, if the terms are decent." Beast's grin is wide, almost hungry. "Things've been a little too quiet around here lately, anyway. We could use a little action."

A couple of the men chuckle and nod. The last few months have definitely been a 'be careful what you wish for' situation. Six months ago, things were pretty damn hot for us.

The Iron Spiders were trying to destroy our club from the south, and the mayor and police department of Tanner Springs were trying to pin anything and everything they could on us. These days — with the Spiders gone underground, and with them the crime and vandalism they brought to our town — shit's been pretty goddamn peaceful.

Too peaceful, maybe.

"Yeah," I nod. "As long as we keep this shit outside of Tanner Springs, I'm good with it."

A few of the other brother grunt their approval. A look around the table shows that many of them seem to be feeling as restless as I am. The Lords aren't built for peace. We thrive on mayhem. On danger.

It's gonna be like old home week around here.

It's probably pretty fucked up that I can hardly wait.

8
ALIX

Because I want to do *something* to thank Gunner for letting me stay at his place for the night, I head to the grocery store to get ingredients to make for spaghetti. I also buy fixings for garlic bread, which sounds really good right now. I still don't know whether he has any plans to come back tonight before dinner. But for simplicity's sake, and because it's cheaper, I decide to get sauce in a jar instead of opting to make it from scratch. Everything that isn't consumed tonight can be saved to be eaten later, either by him or me.

By the time I get back from the grocery store, it's just before five o'clock. I put away the groceries, and then stand for a moment in the kitchen, trying to decide what to do. After the huge breakfast I had this morning at the diner, I was too full to eat lunch. Now it's late enough that I'm finally starting to get hungry again, but early enough that it's not really time for dinner yet. Which means it's still too early to start cooking.

Feeling antsy, I leave the kitchen and go into the living room. Sinking down on the couch, I reflexively pull out my phone and check it for messages, as I've done countless times in the last couple of weeks. First, I look at my texts: nothing. I tap on Eden's name in the history, to glance at the ones I've been sending her practically every day. As always, there's no response — and more depressingly, not even any indication she's read any of them.

I show no new phone calls, either.

For what must be the hundredth time, I consider whether I should try to call her again. Calling is the thing that ends up alarming me most — even more than the texts she doesn't answer. Not only does she never pick up, but the phone always goes straight to voicemail. Which means that either her cell is dead, or she's shut it off. Or maybe she's just blocked me completely. I don't know. But none of these possibilities is good.

With a sinking heart, I decide to try again. Just as I predicted, there's no ring at all. Just a click and her voice telling me to leave a message. Eden sounds happy in her outgoing message — like she doesn't have a care in the world. I know damn well it's not true. It wasn't true when she recorded it, for sure. And even if I don't know where she is or what she's doing, I know what she left behind.

And I know why she left it. At least I think I do.

I just wish I knew she was safe.

I don't bother leaving a message. I've already left six others. If she's listened to them and decided not to call me back, then leaving a seventh won't change anything.

And if she hasn't listened to them...

I don't let myself go there. I've already been down that road too many times. I've already imagined every single possible scenario, from the best case to the worst. It just makes me feel crazy and helpless.

Maybe at least with Gunner's help, I haven't hit a total dead end.

Maybe he really can help me find her. Maybe not. But at least, for right now, I don't feel quite so alone.

To kill some time before I start cooking dinner, I decide to treat myself to a shower.

It's the first real shower I've had in two days, and I'm feeling pretty grimy. I wasn't in that gross motel long enough to take a shower there — and even if I had been, I'm not sure I could have forced myself to climb into that filthy bathtub. It looked like it hadn't been cleaned in this century.

I grab my tiny bottles of shampoo and conditioner off the top of the dresser and take them into Gunner's bathroom with me. The bathroom is small but clean, and the shower stall takes up almost half the space. I was in here earlier, hand washing my dress, but at the time I didn't pay much attention to the shower itself. It's surprisingly luxurious, with a big rainfall shower head and a separate wand thingy that you can use to rinse your hair out with. I sigh in happy anticipation as I poke my head into the tiny linen closet behind the door and pick out a small bath towel. Being careful to make sure the bathroom door is securely closed and locked, I turn on the water and peel off my T-shirt, jeans, underwear, and bra.

The water heats up almost instantly. When I have the temperature adjusted just the way I like it, I step inside the shower and audibly moan at how good it feels. The past couple of days have been woefully short on comfort. Yesterday started with a seven-hour car ride, then devolved into an unfortunate roofie experience, and ended with a night spent passed out on a rock-hard motel bed. Standing here in this steamy shower, the water temperature just exactly right, is almost a religious experience by comparison.

I close my eyes and let the droplets rain down on my skin. It feels so gentle, almost like a caress. In here, locked away from the world, I could almost forget that I'm standing in a strange man's shower, with no idea what I'm doing here or how I'm going to find my sister. I could almost forget my troubles for a while.

Almost.

I stay like that for a few minutes, leaning against the wall and breathing deeply in and out. I try not to think about anything except how amazing it feels. I could probably fall asleep like this if I let myself. Eventually, though, I start to feel guilty for wasting water, so I open my eyes and start focusing on cleaning up. I pull the wrapper off the tiny soap I nabbed from the motel, inspecting it first to make sure it hasn't been used before. Maybe that's paranoid, but I wouldn't put it past that dump. I soap myself up and rinse off, then portion out some of the cheap shampoo and lather it into my hair. The bottle's almost halfway empty by now since I used it to wash my dress, too. I'm going to have to buy more if I plan to stay in the area much longer.

Which it's starting to look like I may have to do.

Worried thoughts about my sister start worming themselves back into my head, but I push them away. *Just for a few minutes*, I tell myself. *Just while I'm in the shower. I'll start worrying about how the hell I'm going to find Eden again once I'm out.*

I rinse out my hair with the hand wand and then apply some conditioner to the ends, working it in and then rinsing that out, as well. Then, all too quickly, I'm done. Regretfully, I turn off the water, and spend longer than I need to toweling off my body and hair. This bathroom feels like an artificial refuge from everything horrible that's happened in my life the past few days. Hell, the past few *months*. Childishly, I wish I could just stay in here, and keep the world at bay.

But of course, I can't. And that's not why I'm here, anyway.

Even though they aren't all that dirty, I don't feel like putting my clothes back on, now that I'm clean. Instead, I wrap the towel around me and gather my jeans, shirt and panties in one hand. At the last minute, I decide to grab the shampoo and conditioner, as well. I don't want Gunner to see them and think I'm planning on staying here any longer than necessary. Awkwardly, I turn the doorknob with my few free fingers and tiptoe out into the hallway toward my room.

"Hey."

Adrenaline instantly shooting through my veins, I shriek loudly and whip around to see Gunner standing in the hallway. *Fuck!* The towel around me is barely large enough to cover what it needs to, and I clutch at it and desperately try to pull it up higher around my breasts. But since I'm also carrying a bunch of stuff, exactly the opposite happens: somehow, I completely lose my grasp on it.

Shampoo and conditioner bottles clatter to the floor, followed by my clothes.

And the towel.

"Well," Gunner grins, licking his lips. "This is one *hell* of a welcome home."

9
ALIX

"*Turn around!*" I yell at him as I bend down and frantically grab at the heap of fabric on the floor. My hands are shaking so badly that I can only paw at it and try to pull it over the most important bits. Above me, I hear Gunner chuckle.

"Turn around?" he rumbles with laughter. "Oh, darlin', not a *chance*."

A roar of embarrassed rage rips from my throat as I leave the shampoo and conditioner behind. I pull the clothes and towel against my chest and crotch and stumble toward my bedroom. Inside, I fling the door closed, the taunting sound of Gunner's chuckling following me. I sit down on the bed, breathing heavily, and try not to cry from embarrassment and shock. *It's not funny!* I want to yell at him, but I know it'll probably just egg him on.

I stay there for countless minutes, frozen in an agony of shame. I have never wanted to disappear into the ether more than I do at this moment. I even contemplate packing up my stuff and climbing out the window. But in the end I know that would just make me feel even more idiotic. And somehow I can't bear the thought of Gunner laughing at me any more than he already is.

I don't even know how long it takes me to pull on some clothes and force myself to open the bedroom door. The only thing that convinces me is knowing the sooner I push past the humiliation, the sooner it will be over.

Out in the living room, Gunner's sitting on the couch with a beer, flipping channels on his TV. He looks over at me and gives me an amused chin lift. "Well, now, darlin'. How was the shower?"

"Fine," I mumble, my face going scarlet.

"Glad to hear it." His eyes leave mine, traveling southward so slowly that I just *know* he's replaying in his mind what he saw a few minutes ago. I don't know how I'm ever going to live down the fact that he knows what I look like naked.

"Are you…" I start to ask *are you hungry*, but I'm afraid he's going to make an off-color joke. And I might just die of embarrassment if he does. "I mean, I, uh, bought some groceries. I thought I could make you dinner. To thank you for letting me stay here tonight."

"Darlin', that show you just gave me was all the thanks I need," he growls. Gunner's eyes visibly darken as they slip back down to rest on my breasts. I feel naked all over again. My nipples tighten in response, heat beginning to pool between my legs.

"Can we please just not talk about that?" I choke. Even more horrifying than being caught naked in his hallway is the fact that I'm actually getting *turned on* by him staring at me like that.

After a long moment, he drags his gaze back up to my face. My expression must convey just how mortified I am right now, because he relents a little.

"Sure thing, darlin'," he drawls. He turns his head back toward the TV. "Doesn't mean I'm not gonna be thinkin' about it, though."

I don't know what to say to that *at all*. So instead, I flee into his kitchen and start searching the cupboards for pots and pans to make dinner. I turn on the oven, and put some water on to boil, hoping that having something to do will make me just the *tiniest* bit less focused on how humiliated I am. While the oven's heating up, I make some garlic butter for the bread. After making scores in the French loaf, I slide the butter between the slices, then put the whole thing on a sheet of aluminum foil that I'm surprised to find in a drawer.

I've just dumped the sauce into the pan to heat up and am getting out a cutting board to chop some vegetables when Gunner wanders in. He sets his empty beer bottle and goes to the refrigerator to grab another. "You want one?" he asks me.

"Sure," I mumble. God, *anything* to take the edge off how nervous I feel around him right now.

He pops the cap off a bottle for me and sets it down next to the cutting board. "Here you go," he says. Then, instead of going back out into the living room, he pulls up a stool to sit down at the kitchen island. I stifle a groan and start cutting.

"What are we having?" he asks in an amused tone.

"Spaghetti," I reply.

"My favorite."

I glance up at him sharply, certain he's making fun of me.

"What?" he asks innocently, spreading his hands. "I mean it. I fucking like spaghetti."

"Good," I say uncertainly. "There's garlic bread, too."

"Even better." He takes a swig of his drink and sets it down. "Can I help?"

I actually start laughing as I try to imagine him chopping veggies. Even him being in a kitchen at all is hard enough to picture — and he's right here so I don't even have to try. "No, that's okay. There's not that much to do." I hold up a small container. "You like mushrooms?"

"I like everything," he replies, raising a brow.

Now that he's seen me naked, practically everything out of his mouth sounds like a sexual innuendo. I force myself to ignore that and start chopping.

"Your knife's dull," I say after a few seconds. "You should sharpen it."

"Yeah, well I don't cook much." He shrugs. "Doesn't get much use." He takes another drink, and thankfully decides to make a stab at a normal conversation. "You have a good day?"

I risk a glance at him. "It was okay. Other than going shopping and..." *And taking a shower...* "Other than going shopping," I continue, reddening, "I didn't do a whole lot."

"Any news about your sister?"

"No." My throat gets a lump in it, and I pick up my bottle of beer and take a drink to clear it. "I've been texting her and calling for days, but no answer. It doesn't even look like her phone is on."

Gunner frowns at me. "So... do you even think she wants to be found?"

I sigh deeply. "I don't know. Honestly, probably not. But I just need to know she's safe. Once I know that for sure, I'll leave her alone if she wants me to."

He's silent for a moment. "What exactly did that fucker Gonzalo tell you at the bar last night? About where your sister is?"

I shrug. "Like I told you before. He said he and Eden

broke up. And she left town. He said he hadn't seen her since."

"And do you believe him?"

"I don't know what to believe." Lifting up the small cutting board, I push the chopped mushrooms into the spaghetti sauce that's simmering in a pan on the stove. "Gonzalo lies like he breathes," I tell him. "Even when he and Eden were together in Lynchburg, he was *always* lying to her. Disappearing and not telling her where he was. Saying he was out with the guys, and then she'd find out later that a friend saw him at a bar with some girl. He was always borrowing money from her, saying he'd pay her back, but he never would." I shrug. "So anything he says is probably bullshit. But he's all I have to go on. And he says she's gone."

For a few minutes, Gunner lets me work in silence. I risk a couple of glances at him; he looks deep in thought. I boil spaghetti, grate parmesan, and get out some plates for us. I figure we'll eat here at the kitchen island, since it's not exactly a fancy dinner. When the food's ready, I hand Gunner his plate and some silverware, then rinse the pasta and let him serve himself.

We concentrate on eating for a while. Gunner pulls off a few slices of the garlic bread and stuffs a piece in his mouth. "This is fucking good," he growls.

I have to laugh. "It's literally just garlic salt and butter. But thanks." It *is* good, actually. Sometimes the simplest meals are the best. It feels oddly therapeutic to just sit down and share a home-cooked meal with someone. I haven't done this in forever. Not since before Mom got sick. A pang of grief hits, me, and I try to ignore it. If I let myself wallow in every sad memory and regret lurking just below the surface, I'd never manage to do anything else.

"So," Gunner says then. "What's your plan for tomorrow?"

Thinking he's trying to find a roundabout way to ask when I'm leaving, I rush to reassure him. "Oh, I promise to be out of your hair. I'll probably just drive back to the bar one last time and hope Eden shows up. If not, I guess I'll drive back to Lynchburg and accept defeat."

There's no way I'm going to give up that easily, of course. But Gunner doesn't need to know that.

"Like hell you will," he barks, as though reading my mind. "You're going to stay here looking for her no matter what. I didn't believe you the first time you tried to feed me that horseshit line, and I don't believe you now. So you might as well admit it now, and let me help you."

"But..." I stammer in frustration, "I've told you before, I don't know how you *can* help me, Gunner. Even if you wanted to. I know literally nothing more than I've told you. My sister's disappeared without a trace, and as far as I can tell, she doesn't *want* to be found. The only hope I have of finding her is if I manage to just run into her somehow, by luck." I shake my head. "And you can't even do *that*. You don't even know what Eden looks like. You wouldn't know her if you passed by her in the street." Despair threatens to overwhelm me. "Plus, you beat up Gonzalo, so he knows who you are now. Even if you went back to the bar looking for him, he'll never talk to you."

"That son of a bitch had it coming," he begins to protest, but I stop him.

"I know," I nod. "And I appreciate it, Gunner. I really do. God knows what he would have done to me if you hadn't stopped him from…" I can't quite bear to finish the sentence. "But even so, be honest. What more can you do to help than you've done already, by getting me away from him and letting me spend the night here?"

"Plenty," he says, a determined look in his eye. "Believe me. But if you want my help — and darlin', trust me when I say you *need* it — you're gonna have to answer some questions and tell me everything I want to know."

10
GUNNER

"Maybe I *should* just give up and go back home," Alix mutters gloomily.

"Come on, darlin'. Don't give up yet. Just tell me more about why your sister left."

We're sitting on opposite ends of my couch after dinner. The house still smells like garlic bread. I'm on my third beer, and Alix is still nursing her second.

I'm still not quite sure why the fuck I'm trying to help her find her sister. She's probably right that Eden has no intention of being found. Still, the broken look in Alix's eyes makes me determined to at least help her get some answers. Even if they end up not being the ones she wants to hear.

"I don't know, exactly," she admits. "I mean, I guess it was just the combination of a lot of stuff. I think maybe all of it ended up being too much for her, so she decided to run away from it." Alix's face turns sad. "Maybe she thought if she could go somewhere new — get a fresh start — all the problems would just go away."

"What kind of problems?" I ask.

Alix heaves a deep sigh, then launches into her story.

"Eden's my older sister, by two years," she begins. "It was just the three of us — Eden, me, and my mom — growing up. My dad lives somewhere out in California, but I've only met him like twice, when I was little. Mom and Eden never got along very well, starting at least from when she was a young teenager. We didn't have very much money, for as long as I can remember. My dad didn't pay child support, and my mom figured it would cost more money and time than she had to try to force the courts to get him to do it. So she just left it alone. Mom had to work two jobs for pretty much my whole life, to keep a roof over our heads."

Alix pauses for a moment, then continues, more softly now. "The two of us girls were mostly left to fend for ourselves when Mom was at work. Since Eden was older, she was in charge of making sure both of us were safe. I guess Mom must have felt guilty that she couldn't keep an eye on us more, because when she did come home, she'd ask us all these questions about exactly what we did while she was gone. She'd grill us about whether we'd left the house, which we weren't supposed to do. If we'd done our homework. Whether we'd opened the door to any strangers. Whether we'd finished the laundry. Stuff like that.

"Eventually, around the time Eden was about thirteen, she started leaving me home by myself when my mom was working her shifts. She'd swear me to secrecy, and tell me she'd beat me up if I didn't lie and say she'd been there the whole time. It didn't take Mom long enough to start getting suspicious that Eden was sneaking out, though. I'm not sure how she figured it out. I never told on her. But even so, I think Eden was convinced that I did.

"By the time Eden was sixteen or seventeen, she and my mom were at each other's throats a lot of the time. And Eden and I had grown apart. She thought I took Mom's side all the time, even though I tried my best to stay out of it." Alex takes a deep breath, then lets it out. "Eventually, Eden graduated from high school. Surprisingly, her grades ended up being really good." She laughs softly. "Do you know, the whole time, she was making the honor roll, and she never once told my mom? It's like she didn't want to give her the satisfaction of knowing there was a smart, responsible girl under all that show of bullshit."

Alix looks so fucking sad, remembering all of this. I almost feel bad for making her tell me, but knowing all this might end up helping me figure out how to find her sister. "What happened then?" I ask.

"For all her complaining about the rules at Mom's house, she didn't move out right away. I was amazed. I thought she'd bolt out of there like a bat out of hell on her eighteenth birthday. But she stayed around." Alix takes a sip of her beer. "She got a part-time job as a receptionist at a salon. Mom made her start contributing a little money toward rent and food. Which was only fair, of course. I was sixteen by then, and I got a job waitressing at a pizza place. For a little while, the financial situation actually eased up a little bit. With the three of us pitching in, we even had a little extra for each of us to have pocket money. Eden and my mom still fought like cats and dogs, but the stress was a little less bad.

"Then, my mom got sick."

Oh, fuck. Alix already told me her mom is dead. I think I know where this story is going.

"The kind of brain cancer she had is called glioblastoma." Alix's voice has gone oddly flat, like she's trying hard not to let any emotion show. "At first, we didn't know anything serious was wrong. She'd been having headaches, and sometimes she seemed kind of foggy after a long day at work. But Mom just chalked it up to being tired. She worked such long hours, after all. She said she wasn't getting any younger, and she just didn't have the energy she used to.

"Eventually, the headaches got worse, and more frequent. To the point where she started having double vision sometimes. She told us they were just migraines, even though she'd never had one before. Sometimes she seemed kind of… confused. Like she wasn't able to think straight. She'd try to hide it from us, but we still noticed. When I tried to talk to her about it, she'd brush me off, or get angry and tell me she just needed to rest.

"Of course," Alix continues, her voice turning bitter,

"Mom didn't have health insurance. None of us did. We couldn't afford it. So she avoided going to the doctor for a really long time." She shakes her head and snorts softly. "Not that it would have done any good, anyway. Glioblastomas basically aren't curable. They're really aggressive, and they even make their own blood supply. By the time they grow enough to start causing symptoms, it's too late. They've invaded the brain tissue enough that the best thing you can hope for is to slow it down.

"Mom refused treatment, saying it made no sense to fight something that would just end up taking her in the end, anyway. She said…" her voice breaks. "She said it was a waste of money."

Alix closes her eyes for a long moment. I want to pull her into my arms but I don't, instinctively knowing she'd pull away. When she opens her eyes again, they're shining with unshed tears.

"Around that time is when Eden started hooking up with Gonzalo." Alix looks at me, disgust evident on her face. "Those last months, when I was doing my damnedest to take care of Mom at home, Eden basically went AWOL. She moved out, and hardly ever came to see us." Her voice turns angry and hard. "At least she came to Mom's funeral," she spits out. "I guess I should be grateful for that, huh?"

"Alix…" I begin. "You don't have to…"

"I don't even know why I'm looking for her, at this point," Alix interrupts me. There's an edge to her tone now, sharp and cutting as glass. "God, it's obvious she wants nothing to do with us, isn't it? With *me*?" She looks hurt, and bewildered, like she can hardly believe what she's doing. "Why the hell am I worried about her?" she asks me, her eyes pleading. "When she obviously doesn't give a damn about me, or about keeping together what's left of our family?"

Fuck. Alix's face is a picture of pure suffering. I don't know what to do or say. I'm a joker. A fighter. Not a goddamn counselor.

But she needs *something*. She's told me all this — revealed more than I ever thought she would to me. And even though I can't know for sure, I doubt she's ever said it to anyone else.

I owe her some kind of a response.

And so I try.

"You're worried about her because she's your sister," I tell her. "Plus, it kinda sounds like she's running from shit she can't face, right into a shitshow she can't control." I shake my head. "That Gonzalo fuck is a goddamn pussy, but he's bad news. You're right to be worried about her."

I think back again to how he roofied Alix, and a wall of pure rage builds up inside me so strong it feels almost like it's going to burst right out of me. I know damn well what that piece of shit was trying to do to her. And if I hadn't been there, he would have gotten away with it. God *damn* it. I can't believe I didn't beat him to death right then and there. My fist clenches so tight my knuckle crack.

If I ever see Gonzalo again, I won't let the opportunity slide a second time.

"I know he is," she whispers. "And I'm scared I won't be able to find her, and get him away from her. And then what if she gets hurt, and I never even know?"

The way she looks at me — not wary or sarcastic, but open and trusting — it fucking *undoes* me. Her eyes turn up to me, soft and wet and vulnerable. When they lock onto mine, something shifts. Her pupils get large, and dark. Her lips part, just a little bit, and her breathing speeds up, rasping a little in her throat. Somehow, while she's been confiding in me, she's dropped her defenses. Her body's turning toward mine, willing and ready.

I stay far the fuck away from any entanglements with women. I've got more than enough shit to deal with in my life as it is.

Last night, I thought I was just afflicted with a rare case of Mr. Good fucking-Samaritan when I dragged her ass out of that bar and onto my bike. This morning, I didn't know what the fuck I was trying to prove by letting her come stay at my place.

I told myself it didn't matter if she's sexy as hell. I'm not a goddamn animal. I can get my needs satisfied anywhere I want. I don't have a thing for damsels in distress.

But it turns out, I was wrong. Somehow, Alix Cousins has dug her hooks into me. Deep. And fuck, I haven't even kissed her.

But that's gonna change. Right goddamn *now*.

11
ALIX

Ever since he surprised me after the shower and I lost my towel, I've been feeling hyper-aware of Gunner's physical presence. There's this… *heat* to him, that practically radiates off of his body whenever he's anywhere in the vicinity. It's like he sends out these sexual waves or something. It's incredibly distracting.

During dinner, it wasn't so bad, because at least there was a kitchen island between us. After we ate, I made sure to scoot as far to one end of the couch as possible, to keep a comfortable distance away from him. But somehow, as he coaxed me into telling him more about Eden, I guess I somehow started moving closer? Or he did? But whatever happened, before I realize it, I look up at him and he's *right there*. His eyes are deep blue. Penetrating. They stare into mine for a few moments, then dip down to look at my lips, which I realize I'm biting in… *anticipation.*

My whole body goes rigid. I'm frozen in my spot.

Because I know if he makes the slightest move toward me, I'm completely lost. I'll let him kiss me. I'll let him do *anything* to me.

God, I want him to do... *everything* to me. *So* badly...

Way back in a corner of my mind, there's a tiny voice that's pleading with me to resist, to move, to do *something* to break the spell. But that voice is drowned out by the louder one — the one that's hammering in my ears, begging him so hard to *touch* me that for a horrible moment, I think I'm actually yelling it out loud.

Slowly, one corner of his mouth goes up in a wicked grin, and I'm *sure* I've said it out loud. But then the grin is gone and his eyes turn wild, almost savage. His voice wraps itself around me like a rope pulling me toward him, and I can't escape — God, I don't *want* to escape.

"Jesus Christ, Alix," he growls low and deep in his throat, almost angrily. "I can't resist you no matter what the fuck I try."

Then his mouth crashes down on mine, and it's not tender, or sweet, or even kind. It's borderline vicious, borderline painful... and *exactly* what I want. A moan rips from my throat as he grabs a fistful of my hair and forces my mouth open, his tongue finding mine and claiming it. Instantly, I'm dizzy, my center of gravity shifting, and then I realize he's lifted me up and brought my whole body down onto him so I'm straddling him. As our mouths devour each other, I feel the hot steel of his need between my legs, pressing against my throbbing core. Gasping at how good it feels, my body takes over, and before I even know what's happening I'm grinding myself against him, my body in control, my mind only a helpless witness to it all.

He unfists my hair and pulls my shirt off over my head in one motion, barely breaking the kiss. Then my bra is off, and he's taken one breast in his large, callused hand. His lips and the rough stubble of his beard slide against the skin of my neck, soft/hard, until he reaches my sensitive nipple and catches it between his teeth. A loud cry rips from me as I jolt against his cock, the pleasure-pain sending an electrical current straight to my core. I'm soaking wet, I can *feel* that I'm soaking right through the fabric of my jeans, and all I can think about is *less fabric, I need less between us, I need to feel the heat of him against my pussy, oh god...* Then my fingers are fumbling clumsily at his waist as I keep grinding against him, trying ineffectually to unbutton his jeans and mine. My brain is frantic, and I'm so close to coming I think it might even happen before I can get any closer to him. He sucks and teases at the tight bud of my areola until I think I might go insane with need. I can hear myself pleading with him, nonsense phrases I just keep repeating with his name, but he seems to know what I mean, because with a grunt he picks me up off the couch and carries me down the hall to his room.

Then I'm on the bed on my back and he's unbuttoning and yanking off my jeans. I lift up my hips and help him. Inside I'm saying *oh, god yes, thank god, oh please oh please...* as he pulls off his shirt and kicks his jeans to the side. His cock springs free, huge and gorgeous, and I think about stopping to take him in my mouth, but then he's on top of me, grabbing my wrists and holding them together over my head.

"This will be my way," he growls, his jaw tight. "Beg if you want."

Then his mouth comes down to nip and suck at my other breast, and I cry out again, writhing underneath him. He teases and teases, his free hand maneuvering the head of his cock to slide against my soaking lower lips and entrance. I gasp again and angle my hips, trying to trick him into sliding partway in, but he yanks roughly up on my wrists, showing me who's boss. I can only wait for him to enter me, to make me come — half out of my mind and my breath rasping painfully in my throat.

He slicks against my painfully swollen clit, over and over. He chuckles low in his throat at my thrashing, loving that he's driving me higher and higher, but refusing to give me what I need. I can hear his breathing speed up, too, and I know he's getting closer. I pray like hell for the moment he'll lose control and have to take me. Finally, just when I think I'm going to go completely insane, he lets out a low, tortured groan and raises himself up.

Gunner reaches down over the side of the bed for his jeans, and then he's rolling on a condom and I want to cry with relief as he slides it on his pulsing shaft. He looks down at me, lids hooded with desire. Our eyes lock for a long moment. The calm before the storm.

Then, with an almost angry growl, he grabs me by the thighs and pulls me roughly toward him, thrusting his hips hard as he enters me all at once.

It's… incredible. I gasp, my eyes flying open and then closing again as the wave of pleasure hits me like a tsunami. He pulls out and thrusts again, and I cry his name, bucking my hips against his. It's explosive, both of us caught in the throes of something larger than the two of us. It's more intense than anything I've ever known. I don't even realize how close I am to the edge again until I'm coming, my whole body shaking and writhing with an orgasm so powerful I'm almost frightened by the force of it, but all I can do is let go and surrender to it. A few seconds later Gunner tenses, then I hear him roar his release. He explodes inside me, thrusting again and again, until he finally slows and stops, both of us completely spent.

We don't speak afterwards. Not for a long time. I'm still gasping for air, so shaken that I'm clutching the bedsheets almost as if I'm afraid I'll fly away if I don't anchor myself to something. Gunner collapses next to me, a wall of heat and mass. For a few moments, I listen to the steady rhythm of his labored breath.

"Fuck me," he mutters.

"Just did," I manage to gasp.

He starts to laugh, so hard he ends up in a coughing fit. "Goddamn it, don't do that. I'm trying to catch my breath here."

"Do what?"

"Be funny."

"Sorry," I say, but I'm smiling. After the intensity of the last few minutes, it's a welcome moment of levity. Also, it's sort of thrilling to hear him laugh and know that it's because of me. It feels sort of *normal*.

Also, it sort of helps to temporarily lessen the awkwardness of the fact that I just had the most amazing, explosive sex ever with a man I barely know

I've never had a one-night stand in my life. I could never understand how a person could just get naked and bump uglies with a person they just met. God, I've never even had sex with someone I wasn't in a relationship with before.

And I sure as *hell* have never had sex that felt *anything* like that.

Is this *normal? Is this what casual sex is like?*

Not according to any of my girlfriends back home, it's not.

So, maybe this is just what it's like with Gunner.

I shiver.

Beside me, he yawns noisily and pulls me to him. "You cold?" he asks. Without waiting for an answer, he yanks the bedspread up to cover both of us, and closes his eyes. A few minutes later, his breathing deepens and slows.

In my head, the fog of sexual satisfaction lifts a little, to give way to a thin thread of worry.

I don't quite know what just happened. I don't know what, if anything, it all means.

And I haven't got the faintest idea how I'm supposed to act around Gunner tomorrow.

12
GUNNER

I wake up in the middle of the night next to Alix, hard as a rock.

Somehow, even though I feel like I just emptied my entire body inside her, I didn't get nearly enough of her the first time around. It's like I've been starving for food and didn't even know it until now.

In the darkness, I pull her sleeping form against me. She stirs and wraps her arms around my neck, then whispers "yes" so urgently that I reach my hand between her legs, parting her thighs to find her wet and ready for me. I stroke her slickened nub until she cries out in pleasure, thrusting and quivering against my hand. Then I push myself inside her again, groaning at how goddamn good she feels pulsing around me, and come so hard I have to stop myself from calling out her name.

The next morning, I'm up before she is.

As I watch her sleep, and think about waking her up to take her again, alarm bells start to go off in my head.

This was probably a mistake. I mean, it felt fucking good as hell, so it definitely wasn't a mistake in that way.

But I can't have Alix thinking what happened last night means more than it does. I don't want her to get the wrong idea.

And it's not just that.

I liked it too much. Way too much.

I don't regret it. Hell, that was the hottest fucking sex I've ever had.

But my dick is starting to fuck with my head a little bit. Alix is addictive. That's not good. I should be fucking women I can take or leave. Which up until now has been all women in the general population, regardless of how hot they look, or how good they are in bed.

Alix moans softly in her sleep and rolls over. A lock of hair falls over her face. I frown and resist the urge to move it so I can look at her some more.

Fuck. I can't have this.

Alix staying here at my place was a bad goddamn idea.

She hasn't even been here one night, and she's already sleeping in my bed.

Not that I begrudge her staying here. Not at all. But if I'm gonna help her, we'll be spending a lot of time together until we get to the bottom of where Eden is. And with Alix, the sex is good. Really, *really* fucking good. And I don't need any complications. Hell, neither does she.

Staying with her here, after tonight — well, that would be a hell of a complication if we got even more tangled up with each other.

I'll sleep at the clubhouse until Alix leaves town, I decide, ignoring the disappointment that floods my head at the thought. I'll let Heather take care of my dick until Alix is gone. To keep the edge off. Heather will fucking love that. She's been doing everything she can to get my attention lately, anyway.

I slide out of bed, take a quick shower, and manage to leave the house before Alix wakes up.

* * *

I'm up early enough that the club's garage isn't even open when I get there.

The garage, Twisted Pipes Custom Chopper and Auto, is our main legit business. At the garage, Hawk's the man in charge. It's his brain child; he built the place from the ground up, with the club's approval. Most of us with any sort of knowledge of bike and auto repair work here — which is all of us. But the custom work we do is the responsibility of a few of the more talented guys. Hawk, Brick, and Ghost do most of the custom engine work. Brick's a fucking wizard with a custom paint job. I do a lot of the shit like twisting pipes on special custom built choppers. Which is what I'm working on now: a set of custom exhaust pipes for a Harley Ironhead XL.

I lose myself in the work for a while. Eventually, other brothers start streaming in. First is Beast, looking like he's coming in from a night of hard drinking. Then Hawk arrives, looking serious and ready to work like always. After him, it's Thorn, with a shit-eating grin on his face that tells me he's ready to greet the day and start bugging the shit out of people just to get a rise out of them. Bullet, one of our newer members, trails in next, looking like he needed about two more hours sleep. Eventually, Geno shows up. He's the club's treasurer, and does all the bookkeeping for the garage.

There's the usual banter and shit-giving. Geno makes some of his piss-water coffee in the office. Brick wanders in about half an hour after Geno. He's brought his own coffee, from his old lady Sydney's coffee shop downtown. He brings in some pastries and shit, too, which Sydney makes in the shop. Predictably, the brothers swarm him as soon as they see the bag he's carrying. Sydney's baking is fucking delicious, and she always makes extra for us.

All the food's demolished in about ten minutes.

The morning passes pretty quickly. With Alix out of sight, it's a little easier for me to force her out of mind, too. At least her body, and what happened last night. Instead, I focus on what she's told me about Gonzalo and her sister, and try to think of a plan.

A little after lunch, Tweak stops by the garage. He doesn't really work here, but stops by sometimes just to hang out and geek out on mechanical and technical stuff. I lift my chin at him and motion him over.

"Hey, brother, good timing. I've got some shit I wanted to talk to you about."

"What's up, brother?" He looks over at the bike I'm working on with an appraising eye. "Nice pipe work."

"Thanks."

"Whadda you wanna talk about?"

"I've got someone I want you to run a check on. Background, location, any priors, who he hangs out with. Any intel you can find on him. Trouble is, I only have one name for him, and I don't know if it's a first or a last. Gonzalo."

Tweak nods thoughtfully. "I can do that. What else do you know about him?"

"Only that he was hanging out at the Smiling Skull over the weekend. I don't think he's a biker, or if he is he wasn't wearing a cut." I pause for a second. "He tried to roofie this chick there. And apparently he had some connection to the chick's sister at one time."

Tweak's radar goes up. "What chick?"

"Keep your dick in your pants," I tell him. "Just some chick from out of town that came looking for the sister, who's gone AWOL."

"And you're helping her?" Tweak's expression is perplexed.

"Yeah," I say flatly. My tone makes it clear that's all I'm gonna tell him about it. "So. Can you get me the intel?"

"Sure, I can do that," he replies. I know wants to ask me more about Alix, but I'm not having it.

"Good," I say gruffly. "Let me know what you find out."

I go back to working on the bike. Tweak asks me a couple more leading questions. I just grunt and keep working. Eventually he wanders away.

* * *

After work, I go into the back and clean up a little. The Lords are having church later, to talk logistics for our upcoming gun run with the Death Devils. But before that, I'm gonna go pay my ma a visit, then stop off at my place and get some shit so I can stay at the clubhouse for the foreseeable future.

It's been a few weeks since I've seen Ma, and I know

from experience there'll be hell to pay if she has to call me and ask me to come over. Ma's a force to be reckoned with when she's pissed.

I ride across town to the small green Cape Cod style house where I grew up. When I get there, a familiar figure in a Lords of Carnage cut greets me out in the front yard.

"Smiley!" I hail him. "The fuck you doing out here?"

"Hey, there, son," he calls back. "Just cleaning out these gutters for your mom."

Smiley's one of the original members of the Lords, meaning he's been there since the club was founded. And since he was a medic in Vietnam, he's our resident doc as well. He's also my ma's ex from way back.

Smiley's actually how I ended up getting involved in the MC in the first place. When Smiley and Ma were dating, way back when I was a young teen, he used to bring me around the club, much to my ma's dismay. After high school, I went into the military, but when I came back I started hanging around the club again, and eventually got patched into the Lords. Smiley and my ma broke up a little while after that. I was never clear on whether my joining the club had anything to do with it. I also could never figure out why the two of them didn't get back together once my ma got used to me being a Lord. Smiley and Ma are clearly crazy about each other, even after all these years. They flirt like hell whenever they're together, and Smiley comes over pretty often to do stuff for her. I suspect he stays over at her place from time to time, too. Plus, since my ma's a nurse, they have a lot of similar knowledge in healing people.

Ma must hear me talking to Smiley, because a couple seconds later she appears at the front door. She's dressed in old blue jeans and a faded Rolling Stones tank top. Her light brown hair, streaked through here and there with gray, is piled up on top of her head in a messy bun. I gotta admit, she looks pretty damn good for being almost sixty years old. Anyone who met her for the first time would think she's in her early fifties at most.

"Ma," I complain as she comes over and gives me a hug. "Why didn't you ask me to do these gutters?"

"Oh, you know. Smiley offered." She shrugs her shoulders and smiles. "I didn't want to bug you. I know you're busy."

"For fuck's sake, Ma, it's no trouble." I glance over at Smiley, who's getting up there both in years and in pounds. "You sure it's a good idea for him to be up on that ladder?" I murmur in a low voice.

"Language," she says with a twinkle in her eye. It's a long-standing joke between us. Ma swears almost as much as I do. "And for God's sake, Gunner. Smiley's *my* age. He's not a damn fossil."

I snort and shake my head, but decide not to push it. "You're right. Sorry. How you doin', Ma?"

"Just fine, like always. Zappa hasn't been feeling too well, though." Zappa's her aging pit bull. "He hasn't been eating as much as usual. Probably have to take him to the vet one of these days soon. Other than that, can't complain."

"Glad to hear it. How's work at the hospital?"

"Good." She nods. "Heading over for a shift this afternoon. I'm covering for Wanda. She's out of town for her son's wedding in Pennsylvania."

"Lucy!" Smiley calls down from atop the ladder. "You might wanna get out of the way. I'm gonna turn on the hose and flush this shit out."

"Come on in the house, Gunner," Ma says, pushing open the screen door. "You want something to eat?"

"Sorry, I can't stay," I apologize. "I just wanted to stop in for a bit and see how you were doing. We've got church in a little while and I gotta run home first."

Ma looks at me skeptically, one hand on her hip. "You mean to tell me you came all the way over here just to pay me a visit for five damn minutes?"

I laugh. "I did. But I promise to come over again in a couple days for longer."

She harrumphs and purses her lips. "Uh-huh."

"I swear."

"Fine," she huffs. "Get out of here, you damn

degenerate." Ma rolls her eyes like she's mad, but I know it's just an act.

I kiss her on the cheek. "See you soon."

She waves me off with an irritated snort and goes back inside. I chuckle and call out to Smiley that I'll see him later at the clubhouse.

13
ALIX

Well, if I was worried about facing Gunner the morning after sex, I didn't have to be. He's gone when I wake up. There's not even a note from him to say good morning or to tell me where he is.

The only indication he's even left — other than the fact he isn't *here*, of course — is a scrap of paper that I find on his kitchen island. It's a phone number. That's all. Since it wasn't here last night, I assume it's Gunner's number. Which means he left it for me on the off chance that I'd need to get hold of him for some reason.

I push the paper aside, angrily and frustrated without even knowing why. What did I expect, a dozen damn roses? Last night was unbelievably amazing, at least for me. The sex was unreal. But I'd have to be a fool to think it meant anything more — for him or for me. He wasn't under any obligation to stick around this morning. And actually, I should be glad he didn't. I ended up telling him way more of my life story than I'm comfortable with last night. It's just as well that I didn't have to face him over the breakfast table today.

I rummage in a cupboard for the rest of the bread I bought yesterday, then make myself some toast and coffee, which I consume sitting at the kitchen island while staring into space.

Gunner told me he was going to help me find Gonzalo. But we never got to the part about *how*.

Trust me, he said.

I guess I have to trust that he hasn't forgotten his promise. And that it wasn't just a line he was using on me to get me into bed.

Strangely, I *do* kind of trust him — about that, anyway. I believe he's going to *try*. And the more I think about it, it's true that he probably does have a better chance of finding anything out than I do. For one thing, he's *from* here. He's definitely got more connections than I do. For another thing, he's a man. And a large, strong, dangerous-looking man at that. People are likely to take him a lot more seriously than they are me. I need to face facts: whether I like it or not, Gunner's my best bet to getting answers about where Eden is.

Which means it looks like I'm going to be staying here in Tanner Springs — and at his house — a little while longer.

Once I've finished doing my dishes and putting them in the little rack next to the sink, I glance back over at the kitchen island, to the paper with his number on it. Reluctantly, I pull out my phone and punch it into my contacts. After all, Gunner is basically the only person I know within a four-hundred mile radius, and this number is my only link to him. Last night notwithstanding, I should be grateful that he was thoughtful enough to leave it for me.

After breakfast, I turn anxiously in circles in the house, not knowing what to do with myself. It's driving me a little crazy that this isn't my space, and I don't have any of my stuff with me. All I can do is wait for Gunner to come back so we can talk more about *how* he plans to help me track down Eden.

In the meantime, though, there is one thing I do need to do. A call I was hoping I wouldn't have to make. But at this point, I know it's inevitable.

Going out to sit on Gunner's front porch, I search in my phone for the number I want, and press the call button. A couple of rings later, someone answers on the other end.

"Valuland Grocery," a familiar female voice says.

"Renee?" I answer? "This is Alix. Is Todd there?"

"Hey, girl," Renee says cheerfully. "Yeah, he's here. Hold on a minute."

Renee puts me on hold, and I listen absently to the staticky muzak, interspersed with short ads about our weekly specials on vegetables, canned goods, and meats. About a minute later, there's a loud click as the phone picks up.

"Valuland, this is Todd."

"Hi, Todd, this is Alix."

"Hey." My manager's voice is clipped and suspicious, almost as though he already suspects what I'm about to say.

"So..." I begin, inwardly cringing. "I'm calling to ask if I can get a couple more days off. I'm still out of town, and I, uh... well, things have gotten a little more complicated than I thought they would be."

"Alix," Todd says in an irritated tone, "I already arranged your schedule to give you two days off in a row."

"I know, I know," I agree hastily. "And I appreciate it. I just need a few more days. Three, max. I'll even switch shifts with anyone who's available. I just..."

"Alix, I'm not going to point out how lucky you are to have enough hours to get benefits," he interrupts. "Half the cashiers in this store would kill to have as many hours as you do."

"I know, but..."

"I'll give you one more day."

"But that's not..."

"No buts," he says, cutting me off impatiently. "If you can't get it together after tomorrow, I'm giving your hours to someone else."

I try to argue with him, but Todd's not having it. Never mind that I've worked at Valuland more than a year, and until now, I've never once asked for so much as an hour off from the schedule he sets — not even when my mom died. Never mind that he knows how much I need this money. He just doesn't care, and I know I can't make him.

I hang up the phone dejectedly, the full weight of what this means hitting me.

I'm basically going to be fired from Valuland.

Screw it, I think irritably. *It's not like working as a grocery store cashier is my life's ambition.*

And it's not like the money I make there has been enough to save Mom's house, anyway.

That ship has sailed. Foreclosure proceedings started not long after she got diagnosed. Without Eden's help, there's nothing left to be done. One way or another, the house is going back to the bank soon.

Which means my last reason to go back to Lynchburg before finding my sister just evaporated into thin air.

Fuck it. I'm in Tanner Springs for the duration. Eden may

not want to talk to or hear from me, but she's the only family I have left. One way or another, I'll pursue this to the end. I *will* find out where my sister is and what's happened to her, no matter what it takes. After that, I'll cross the next bridge when I come to it.

For hours, I wait for Gunner to come back or call me. I try to watch soap operas on TV. I flip through some of his paperbacks. I just barely resist snooping through his stuff in search of more information about who he is.

In the end, I last until a couple hours after lunch time. When he *still* hasn't called by almost three o'clock, I jump up and make my decision.

I can't stand it anymore.

I'm done waiting around twiddling my thumbs for Gunner to get home. Who knows how long it will take for him to get around to helping me, after his club business is taken care of? I've never been able to rely on anyone but myself in the past, and I'm not going to waste any more precious time doing it now.

Grabbing my purse from the coffee table and Gunner's keys from the hook by the door, I step outside and lock the house behind me.

It's time for a road trip. I have exactly one idea of a lead on tracking down Gonzalo again, and I'd rather do that than sit here doing nothing, even if it gets me nowhere. If I'm lucky, I'll have just enough gas in my tank to get me to the

Smiling Skull bar and back to Tanner Springs.

14
GUNNER

When I show up at my place to grab some clothes and shit before church, Alix's car is gone and she's nowhere to be found.

At first, I think she's changed her mind about staying here and she's skipped town. I call out her name as I stride through he living room, swearing loudly in the silent house. I'm pissed at myself for not getting her cell number before I left the house today. *Stupid mistake, you dumb fucker. You should have known there was a chance she might run after last night.* My mind is racing wildly, wondering how the fuck I'm going to figure out where she's gone, when I stop suddenly at the doorway to the second bedroom.

There, sitting on the dresser, are some small travel bottles of shampoo and conditioner, a paperback, and a hairbrush.

The sight of such ordinary objects — just the normalcy of how they look sitting there — calms me down almost immediately.

I take a deep, relieved breath and open the top drawer of the dresser. A few shirts, a couple pairs of panties, some socks.

In the bathroom, the simple white dress is still drying on the towel rack.

"Jesus," I mutter, running a rough hand through my short hair. I'm a little weirded out by how worried I was that she'd left. I go into the kitchen to grab a glass of water. Glancing over to the counter of the kitchen island, I notice the scrap of paper I wrote my number on.

Rummaging in a nearby drawer for a pen, I scrawl a quick note under the number:

Staying at the clubhouse tonight. I'll see you tomorrow and we'll talk about finding your sister.

I've got a guy working on intel about Gonzalo. Text me when you see this. - G

This way, I kill three birds with one stone. She'll know she's safe staying here tonight; I'll know when she comes back here; and I'll get her phone number, which I should have fucking done in the first place.

Going back down the hall to my room, I grab a small duffel bag and fill it with a couple of changes of clothes to take with me. Then I head over to the clubhouse.

Later, in church, Rock goes over the final details of the run we'll be doing with the Death Devils, including which of us will be going. The run is no more dangerous than usual, as far as gun exchanges are concerned, but Oz has asked for six Lords to back up his club. Rock chooses which ones of us will go. He's not coming with us, as having two MC presidents there might be perceived as a challenge to Oz's authority and a sign of weakness in front of their connections, especially because they used to do business with us. Angel is going with us in his place.

Rock tells us what time we'll be heading out the next day. Then he bangs the gavel, and church is over.

"The men seem pretty keyed up about this run," Angel observes as we file out of the chapel.

"Yeah," I chuckle. "I think some of them miss the thrill of gun running."

"You?" Angel asks, cutting his eyes to me with a grin.

"I can't deny, booze and pussy taste especially good when there's a little danger on the other side."

Angel laughs out loud. "You got that right. Matter of fact," he continues, eyeing a couple of the club whores, "I think I'm gonna test out that theory right now."

He ambles over to Melanie and Tammy, who are more than pleased to get the attention of the club's esteemed vice-president. They immediately jump to their feet and teeter toward him on their heels, hands sliding under his leather cut and over the crotch of his jeans. Angel grabs each of them by the ass and then nods toward the stairs leading to the apartments on the second floor. On the way, he nabs a bottle of whiskey from the bar to take up with him.

"They look like they're having fun," Heather's voice croons in my ear. "Wanna do likewise?"

"Heather," I mutter, "this ain't anything other than…"

"I know, I know," she smirks prettily. "I'll take what I can get." Turning up the corners of her cherry-red lips in a seductive little smile, she breathes, "I need your cock, Gunner. Give me what I need, baby."

It's not really what I want — because truth be told, what I want is more of Alix. But I tell myself that the best way to get that girl out of my mind is to remind myself that Alix was just sex, nothing more. No matter how fucking good it was.

A little roughly, I grab Heather's arm and lead her upstairs, trying to ignore her little coos of excitement. When we get up there, I pull her into my apartment and shut the door. Immediately, she's down on her knees, unzipping my fly.

I close my eyes and frown, trying to push Alix out of my

thoughts.

But all that happens is her face appears right in front of me. Her eyes flutter closed, her arms wrapping around my neck as she whispers, "Yes…"

My cock is immediately hard as a steel bat. Which Heather attributes to her feminine wiles.

"Oh, baby," she moans. "Yeah, I've missed your cock…"

Fuck. I'm not up for this. The last thing I want right now is Heather sucking me off, much as I hate to admit it.

I pull her up forcefully, ignoring her cry of protest, and haul her to her feet. "Sorry, babe, ain't happening tonight."

"But why!" she mewls in protest. "You know you want me." She reaches out and palms my hard shaft. "I can make you feel so good, Gunner. You know how good I can make you feel…"

"Enough!" I grab her wrist so abruptly she yelps a little. "I said we're done here." I nod my head toward the door. "Get out," I say angrily.

"But…"

"Out!"

With a last reproachful glance, Heather wobbles out the door on her stilettos and closes it behind her. I almost feel bad. I'm not exactly angry at her, though she's not very good at taking no for an answer.

I'm mad at myself.

For fucking Alix in the first place.

And for thinking Heather — or any other girl — would be just as good. Like Alix was just another place to stick my dick.

Alix is way fucking more than that.

And if I'm not careful, she's gonna be an addiction.

Locking the door, I check my phone, but she hasn't texted me yet. I frown and try to turn my thoughts to something else, but it's no use. I'm still painfully hard, and that ain't gonna change by itself.

I liberate my pulsing cock from my jeans and lean against the wall, closing my eyes. I know I shouldn't do this and think of her, but fuck it. I'm too far gone. I stroke myself, as slowly as I can stand it, and imagine instead that I'm pushing myself deep inside Alix as she moans and writhes for me. I can hear her voice, hear that hitch in her throat before she cries out and starts bucking against me. *Jesus.* That's all it takes. With a loud groan I shoot my load, the force of it almost painful.

This is bad, I think when it's all over.

Staying away from Alix is gonna be a lot harder than I thought.

Back downstairs, I ignore Heather's attempts to make me jealous by falling all over any Lord who'll give her a second glance. I decide I'm gonna concentrate on drinking away my troubles. I grab a bottle of Jack and a shot glass from Jewel and go over to smoke Lug Nut at pool a couple of times.

Midway through the first game, I finally get a text from Alix. But it's not what I expect.

> Having some car trouble. Can you help?

Instead of texting back, I punch the call back number and wait for her to pick up. She answers on the second ring.

"What's up?" I growl.

"I'm stuck out here on the highway," her apologetic voice comes over the line. "I'm not sure what's wrong with my car, but it's overheated and I don't have any water or anything to put in it. And it's starting to get dark. Could you come pick me up?"

"Out where?" I repeat. "Where are you?"

Alix hesitates. "I'm on Highway Twelve," she finally tells me. "About fifteen miles west of the Smiling Skull."

15
ALIX

Even over the phone, I can tell Gunner is furious.

Dammit. I never intended to even tell him about this trip, unless something useful came out of it. I knew he'd be angry and try to stop me from going if I'd let slip what I intended to do. And on one level, I can't blame him. But I just couldn't stand not doing anything. I've never been good at waiting around for things to happen.

The trip east toward the Smiling Skull was uneventful. I showed up at the bar a little after five p.m. with only the vaguest notion of what I was going to do. The parking lot was almost half-full, with twice as many bikes as cars. I pulled in and shut off my car, then, steeling myself, I walked resolutely toward the front door.

Inside, an iron-jawed, angry-looking bartender with a

shaved head watches me walk up, suspicion etched on his rough features.

"You sure you're in the right place, blondie?"

"Is Rosie around?" I ask, with much more confidence than I feel. "I need to talk to her."

He snorts. "You don't know Rosie," he mutters, turning away.

In desperation, I decide to take a chance. "Gunner sent me! From the Lords of Carnage." The bartender turns back to me with a dubious expression. "He told me Rosie would help me out," I explain.

He clearly doesn't believe me, but at this point I'm guessing he just wants me out of his hair — or lack thereof. Picking up a phone, he punches a button and murmurs into it. Hanging up, he narrows his eyes at me. "She'll be out in a second. You want a fuckin' Shirley Temple while you're waiting?"

I decide to ignore the insult. "I'm fine, thank you."

By this time, some of the other customers are looking at me with the same curious and contemptuous expression as the bartender. I can't help but think back to that first night when I was here looking for Gonzalo. I suppress a shudder, recognizing that this really is not a safe place for me to be by myself.

An old woman comes out into the bar area. She's short

— at least an inch shorter than I am — and looks to be in her late sixties, at least. She's thin to the point of emaciation, and wearing a white shirt, a black vest, and a red bandana around her neck. Her no-nonsense silver hair is cut short and severe. Frankly, if I met her on the street I wouldn't immediately be sure if she was a man or a woman. *This* is Rosie?

She seems as skeptical of me as I am of her. "Who the hell are you?" she asks bluntly, in a raspy smoker's voice.

"Gunner Storgaard sent me," I say, working hard to sound confident. "He said you might know something about a person I'm looking for."

"That so?" she snaps. "Well, if Gunner needed information, why the fuck didn't he come here himself?"

"He… he's helping me out," I explain hastily. "He's a friend of mine."

Rosie throws back her head and cackles. "Honey, Gunner don't have friends. Especially friends without dicks."

"Well, anyway," I stumble, reddening. "He *is* helping me. And he told me you might be able to tell me where Gonzalo is."

Out of the corner of my eye, I think I see a couple of people glance at me, but I can't be sure.

"Gonzalo?" Rosie's voice is sharp. "Why the fuck would I know where that asshole is?"

"I just thought… he might have been here recently. Or you might know where he lives. Or something." I trail off, feeling idiotic.

"'Or something.'" Rosie mocks my tone, cackling again. "Look, girly," She takes a step closer, putting a gnarled fist on her hip. "I don't know what you're about, and I don't give a shit. I don't know you from a hole in the ground, and I've got shit to do. If I were you, I'd get the hell out of here."

"But if you could just tell me whether…"

The bartender suddenly appears at Rosie's side. "You speaka da English?" he booms at me, poking his finger aggressively to the side of his head. "Rosie told you to get the hell out!"

A hatchet-faced man with long, greasy hair seated at the bar chuckles loudly. When I glance over at him, he shoots me an aggressively sexual leer.

I open my mouth to reply to Rosie, but stop. I realize no one here is going to tell me a damn thing. And I'm starting to feel very uncomfortable, and very conspicuous. The longer I stay, I realize, the more likely it is that something bad will happen to me.

"Okay. I'm leaving," I murmur, taking a step backwards. I'm almost a little afraid to turn my back, but I force myself to do it, and walk out of the bar as calmly as I can. Outside, I realize my heart is pounding. My hands are trembling, half from fear and half from anger. I'm mad at them for being so mean, and mad at myself for being fool enough to have come here.

Back in my car, I lock the doors and take a few deep breaths to calm myself. This whole thing was a total bust. Closing my eyes for a moment, I try to think whether there's any way I can salvage anything from this trip. There's a town just to the east of here. Maybe I should just take a chance and go drive around, hoping I happen to see something? Maybe I'll...

Thump! Thump! Thump!

I shriek in fright and jump in my seat, banging my head on the ceiling of the car. Wildly, I turn toward the noise to see the hatchet-faced guy from the bar leering at me from the other side of the driver's side window. He's grinning and laughing, obviously happy he scared me. Before I realize what he's doing, he reaches for the door handle. I scream, turning the key in the ignition, The car roars to life. I know I locked the doors but I'm still terrified that somehow he might get in. I slam the car into reverse and hit the gas, not caring whether I run over him or not. He yells angrily and pounds on the hood of my car. I throw it into forward and squeal out of the lot, barely looking to see if there's oncoming traffic as I hit the highway and drive away as fast as I can.

For a few seconds all I can do is try not to hyperventilate or crash the car as I accelerate, glancing in my rear view mirror several times to make sure no one's following me. Eventually, as I continue back in the direction of Tanner Springs, the panic starts to dissipate little by little. What takes its place is a wave of despair, as I realize that for the second time I've walked all alone into a dangerous situation like a complete idiot. And for all that, I'm no closer to finding out anything about my sister.

I've never felt so helpless and stupid in my life.

It seems the fates aren't done with me, though, because not long after I'm out of town, the car's temperature light comes on. I down at the temperature gauge, and see the car is seriously overheating. Swearing, I pull over to the side of the road and reach down to put the car in park. As I do, I realize I've been driving in low gear all this time.

"God DAMN it!" I yell, pounding my fist on the steering wheel.

I'm stuck. I don't know anything about cars. I'm afraid to drive any farther, and I have no idea what to do next.

Worst of all, I know — even though it's the *last* thing I want to do — that I'm going to have to call Gunner to come help me.

A little over half an hour later, a tow truck arrives. The driver's side door opens, and Gunner climbs out. I unlock my doors to get out and meet him.

The first thing I noticed is how pinched and angry-looking his face is.

"Thank you *so* much for coming, Gunner," I begin, but he brushes past, barely looking at me.

I watch in helpless silence as he goes to my car, gets into the driver's seat, and turns it on. He checks the instrument panel, then turns it back off. Sliding back out, he pops the hood, spends a minute or so looking around inside, and then slams it shut, hard. In spite of myself, I jump.

"Get in the truck," he barks. Beneath the beard, his jaw clenches. Swallowing hard, I do what he says, climbing up into the high cab and shutting the door. I watch from the inside as Gunner positions a metal chain cradle under the front wheels. He lifts them up with a winch on the truck, then checks to make sure everything's hooked up correctly. All the while, I'm sitting in the passenger seat, my hands clenched together and dreading the moment when he finally gets in the cab with me.

But the firestorm I'm expecting doesn't come. When he's finished, Gunner climbs in and turns on the tow truck's engine without a single glance at me. He pulls out onto the highway, shifting gears as he speeds up, and soon we're on our way back to Tanner Springs. The whole way home, he doesn't say a single word. It's like I'm not even there.

This is a million times worse than if he had just yelled at me like I was expecting.

The ride seems to last forever, but eventually we hit the city limits. Once we get into town, he drives me straight to his house and pulls up to the curb. Putting the truck in park, he finally turns to me.

"Your car is fucked," he grunts. "I'm taking it to our shop."

"Gunner —" I begin.

"*Go inside*," he orders, his face contorted into a snarl.

"Thank you," I whisper helplessly, and open the passenger door.

I've barely slid out of the cab when he reaches over to slam the door roughly behind me. He puts the truck in gear, and roars off into the evening.

I'm left standing dejectedly on the sidewalk, knowing he won't be back again tonight.

Every single decision I've made today was the wrong one.

Tiredly, I drag myself up the front walk and into the house. I just want to go to bed.

Maybe things will be better tomorrow morning.

In any case, they can hardly be worse.

16
GUNNER

The next day, I wake up in my apartment at the clubhouse, restless as hell and ready for action.

It was all I could do last night to not lose my fucking shit on Alix. I couldn't even ask what she was doing out there on that highway because I was so fucking furious. I know she went to the Smiling Skull to look for Gonzalo again. I can't believe she'd be so goddamn stupid, after what almost happened last time.

Well, at least for now, I've nipped that problem in the bud. She's carless now. And she will be for the foreseeable future, since that's the only way I can make sure she doesn't get it into her head to go off looking for Eden by herself again.

All her overheated car needed was coolant. I was pretty sure that's what the problem was when I talked to her on the phone. I even brought some with me in the tow truck. But on the way to get her, I realized I could keep her car in the shop if I told her it was a more serious problem. If she wants to go back to the Skull again now, she's gonna have to hitchhike. And I don't think even Alix is crazy enough to do that.

Last night I was so goddamn mad I didn't trust myself to even talk to her. Shit, she could have gotten herself seriously hurt. She could have wound up in the exact same boat as her sister — wherever the hell that is. Then I'd have two women to rescue instead of one.

The thought of Alix disappearing makes my blood turn to ice in my veins.

I'm still fucking furious with her this morning. But as I take a shower as cold as I can stand it and pull on some clothes, I grudgingly start to wonder whether I'm partly to blame for her going off like that. I know Alix has been stuck waiting at my place with no news. And I know she feels like the clock is ticking on finding her sister. I realize I haven't been all that great about communicating with her. Tweak's been doing everything he can to track down the intel we need to find Gonzalo, but Alix doesn't know that. She's probably been going out of her mind with worry.

As stupid as her little stunt was yesterday, I have to admit I probably had a small part in it.

Just before I go downstairs to grab some coffee and breakfast, I take my phone out and thumb a quick message to her, so she'll at least know I'm not gonna leave her hanging for another day.

> I'm going on a run with the club. I'll talk to you later on today

I'm midway through breakfast when I get a response from her:

> I'll try to fit you into my busy schedule.

I can't tell if she's mad or not. She might be mad.

Well, too fucking bad, I think irritably. *I'm mad, too.*

Sighing, I shove the phone in my pocket and take my cup out into the main room of the clubhouse.

I go find Angel and ask him what time we're leaving on the run. He tells me that it's been postponed for a couple of hours, so I go outside and spend a little time making sure my bike is tuned up and ready to go. When I'm finished, I figure I'll go see if Tweak has had time to get any of the intel I asked him for. I wander through the bar area and into one of the back rooms that Tweak has set up as his command station. He's there, sitting at a desk surrounded by three large, flat-screen computer monitors, tapping away and lost in thought.

"Hey," I murmur, pulling up a chair and flipping it

around so I can lean my arms across the back of it. "You had any time to work on finding out about that Gonzalo fucker?"

"Good timing," he replies, barely looking up. "I was just checking into some stuff. Haven't had a lot of time yet to dig." He motions me closer. "That him?"

I peer at an image on the far monitor. "Yeah. That's him." It's a mug shot. I look closer. "Gonzalo Medina," I read. So Gonzalo's his first name, not his last. "What did he get busted for?"

Tweak snorts. "What hasn't he been busted for? Drug possession, felony theft, aggravated assault. I got a feeling I'm just getting started."

I nod. "You got his twenty yet?"

"Not yet. But I'm pretty sure he lives in the area. Apparently he grew up around here. In Death Devils territory."

His words give me an idea I hadn't thought of before. "Okay," I grunt. "Let me know when you have an address for him. And call me right away if you find out anything else important."

Tweak tears his eyes away from the screen to look at me. "Like what?"

"No idea," I admit. "Anything that makes your eyebrows go up. Remember we're looking for the sister of this chick I'm trying to help."

"So, about this chick…" he begins. "I might have more to go on if you bring her in here, so I can ask her some questions myself." He gives me a knowing smirk. "But if you don't wanna share her with the club, that's fine by me."

"Fuck you, Tweak," I snarl, my anger getting the better of me before I can stop it. "Alix ain't a club whore. I don't want her here at the clubhouse with you filthy motherfuckers."

"Whoa, whoa, whoa." Tweak scoots his chair away from the computer, holding up his hands. "Calm yourself, brother. Shit, I didn't know you were so serious about her." He gives me a look I can't quite read. "You claimin' her? Because you know damn well no one's gonna touch what's yours. You give the word, she'll be safer here than anywhere else."

"I'm not claiming…" *Goddamnit.* "It ain't like that, Tweak. I just want to make sure she's protected. I'm doin' her a favor, and I'm not gonna let her get hurt or used on my watch."

"Shit, Gun," he protests. "You know all you gotta say to the men is she's off limits."

I know he's right. My brothers would never touch her as long as I say the word. Still, it doesn't sit right with me, bringing her here. Having the other Lords ogling her like she's a piece of meat.

Tweak is right, though. I should probably bring her in. It doesn't make any sense not to let him ask her questions directly.

Six Lords meet the Death Devils at an agreed-upon spot between our clubhouses. Then our two clubs set out riding south, toward the Kentucky border. We're picking up a shipment of guns from a cartel that our club used to do business with. Once we pick them up, we'll be bringing them to a warehouse in Devils territory that they own, to be stored there until the Devils can arrange a meet-up with the organization they're selling the guns to.

Oz tells us the shipment is three crates of pistols that are coming up to us from Florida, by way of Atlanta. The Lords are providing the security on both ends: both the pickup and the delivery. The terms of the arrangement have been negotiated between Rock and Oz. Part of our compensation's financial. The other part is mutually-assured partnership in the future, against any potential enemies to one or the other of our clubs.

We get to the pickup spot in the mid-afternoon. It's a secluded place out in the country, in a densely wooded area that makes me a little jittery. There's lots of cover where armed men could hide, and I find myself scanning the landscape for the slightest sign of movement. The Lords of Carnage had a business relationship with this cartel, called the Crow Clan, for many years. But we never met up here before.

I can tell Angel and Ghost are thinking the same thing as I am as we climb off our bikes. Angel shoots me a warning look and I lift my chin just slightly to acknowledge it. We've driven in with a group of Devils on bikes just behind a dark blue panel van that will transport the crates back to their warehouse.

Kane, the head of the Crow Clan, looks surprised and more than a little suspicious to see the Lords pulling up with the Death Devils.

"Gentlemen," he says in a subdued, rasping voice that I know only too well. A deep, jagged scar on his throat, long since healed, betrays the source of his strange croak. "It's been a long time since the Lords of Carnage have graced our presence. To what do I owe the pleasure?"

Instead of answering, Angel looks over at Oz, letting him take the lead.

"The Lords happened to be in the neighborhood," Oz says pleasantly. "They thought they'd come say hello."

Kane snorts, his eyes flicking from the Devils to the Lords. "A fuckin' party."

"You may have heard that a few of our men are indisposed at the moment," Oz continues, a slight edge in his voice. "The Lords have agreed to provide some extra security in their absence."

Kane sneers slightly. "Hope you can hold on to these guns once they're in your hands, Oz," he rasps. "Though, that's not really my problem."

"No. It's not," Oz agrees coldly. "Speaking of which." He crosses his arms in front of him. "Shall we get down to business?"

If Kane is pissed that Oz doesn't want to sit around jawing all day, he doesn't show it. He motions to a couple of his men. "Bring the crates," he hisses. They turn back toward an old, battered pickup truck that has the logo of a plumbing company on the side panels. Opening up the back of the covered truck bed, they slide out three crates, one by one, as the rest of us watch in silence. Around me, I can feel the alertness of the other Lords, at the ready in case of anything unexpected.

"Open the crates," Oz orders once they're set in front of us. Kane's men do as he says.

Oz's Sergeant at Arms and Vice-President move forward to take a look. They each pull out a gun to examine them. Even from here, I can tell they're not the quality the Lords was used to getting from them.

"These are shit," Oz's VP growls. "You couldn't get two-hundred dollars for these on the open market."

"Maybe so," Kane rasps. "But they'll easily sell for five or six-hundred dollars in New York City."

He's right. The markup on these guns in NYC could easily be upwards of five-hundred percent. I don't know who Oz is selling these guns to, though I'm assuming it's to one of our former customers. Maybe they'll be happy with these pistols. Either way, it ain't my place to judge, and I couldn't care less, as long as the deal goes through without incident.

Oz's VP brings him the pistol he's been examining. Oz racks it, sights it, and nods briefly. "And the ammo?"

"It's all there," Kane affirms.

Oz nods to his VP, who takes the pistol back from him and tosses it in the crate. From inside the van, one of Oz's men appears with a dark-colored duffel, and hands it to Kane. Kane nods at one of his men, a large, squarish guy with crude features, to take it. He holds the bag up at Kane's chest level to let him open it and examine the contents.

After a few seconds, he nods. "Okay. We're good."

Next to me, I hear Ghost exhale slightly.

"Gentlemen." Oz looks around the room once. "It's been a pleasure."

He turns to go, and his men follow behind him. The Lords stay in position, watching Kane and his men until they've piled into their vehicles and moved out onto the deserted gravel road. As they retreat into the distance, Angel nods at us and we break formation.

The Death Devils and the Lords make our way back to our bikes and the large van. As we do, I decide to take a chance. "Oz," I call. "Can I have a word?"

It's unusual for a patch holder of one MC to approach the president of another MC without the explicit direction of his own prez. But this ain't about club business. This is personal. And Oz may be able to give me information that no one else can. Angel shoots me a look but I ignore it.

Oz stops in his tracks and turns to me. Clasping his hands in front of him, he stands at attention, like a statue. It's a demeanor I've seen him adopt many times, though I barely know Oz. He's famously hard to read. Impassive to the point of strangeness, until he's pushed past his breaking point. I don't know this from experience, but I've heard stories. You do not want to fuck with Oz Mandias.

"Yes?" he says, in a polite but distant tone.

"I'm looking for some information on a punk ass thug who may live in your territory. Name's Gonzalo Medina."

He stares at me for a long moment.

Then he blinks once.

"Yes?"

"You know him?"

He reaches up to stroke his long, salt-and-pepper beard. His expression doesn't change. "I know him."

"What can you tell me about him?"

Oz's eyes bore into me. "Is there a reason why I should give you this information?"

"It's personal," I admit. "Not club business. I know you don't owe me shit. But Gonzalo might have the sister of a friend of mine. She's disappeared and we don't know where she is." I meet his gaze. "If you could point me in the right direction — any direction — I'd appreciate it."

Oz's expression flickers just an imperceptible hair when I mention Alix's sister. He opens his mouth, measuring his words.

"Medina's crew is based out of Red Hawk," he finally tells me in a clipped voice. "They deal mainly in heroin. Shit quality, sold to junkies who are so desperate they'll take anything." He hesitates. "They have a reputation for violence where women are concerned. And use of drugs for *compliance*. If your friend's sister is with him, she either enjoys that sort of thing, or…" He waits a beat. "She does not."

Fuck. This is worse than I thought. I think back to Gonzalo trying to drug Alix, and my blood boils as I realize he might not have only been trying to drug her for his own pleasure. The full extent of what might have happened to her if I hadn't seen it and intervened hits me like a baseball bat.

If Eden is still with Gonzalo, she's in a world of danger.

And one thing is clear: I have to be careful how much of this I tell Alix. It would kill her to know what her sister might be facing.

I need to find Eden as soon as I can, and hope it's not too late.

"Do you happen to know where their HQ is located?" I ask Oz.

"I don't personally concern myself with the likes of Medina and his crew," he murmurs, a look of distaste briefly distorting his features. "But they should not be difficult to find in Red Hawk."

"Thank you," I say.

The president of the Death Devils nods mildly and turns away. The conversation is over.

"What the hell was that about?" Angel asks.

"A personal matter," I tell him. "He knows somebody I'm looking for."

"Is that right?" He frowns. "Is this something the club should know about?"

"Probably." I look Angel in the eye. "I'm gonna need to ask for some help from the Lords."

Angel's demeanor instantly changes. "You know we got your back, brother. Anything you need, we're there."

I lift my chin. "I know." Glancing at the others, I continue. "But I'm not too sure Rock's gonna be happy about what I'm asking. I'm gonna need to bring someone to the club. The sister of the woman I'm looking for. She needs help."

"She someone from Tanner Springs?" Angel eyes me

curiously.

"No." I shake my head. "I'll tell you more later. Right now, let's get back to town. After what Oz just told me, I don't want to waste any more time."

17
ALIX

I wake up the next morning to the depressing prospect of spending another whole day hanging around Gunner's house. Within half an hour of getting up, I am already going completely and utterly stir-crazy.

Back in Lynchburg, I never seemed to have even a moment to myself. Between working as many hours as I could scrape together at Valuland, taking care of mom while she was sick, and trying really hard to keep up on paying bills and not losing the house, I could have used roughly thirty-six hours in every day.

And even then, I probably would have only managed about four hours of sleep a night.

But here in Tanner Springs, with all sorts of time on my hands and nothing to do but wait? Every minute seems to last an hour. And now I don't even have a damn car anymore.

It's not until I go into the kitchen for some breakfast that I see the note Gunner left for me on the counter underneath his phone number.

Staying at the clubhouse tonight. I'll see you tomorrow and we'll talk about finding your sister.

I've got a guy working on intel about Gonzalo. Text me when you see this. - G

He must have come here looking for me when I was on my way to the Smiling Skull yesterday.

He wasn't angry with me then.

God. Everything is *so* fucked up.

I'm slogging through a meal of cold cereal and feeling generally sorry for myself when my phone buzzes. It's Gunner. The text is brief, and neutral.

I'm going on a run with the club. I'll talk to you later on today

Later on today. Great. That could mean anything.

Even though I'm still feeling chastised from last night,

I'm frustrated enough that I can't help but send him a snarky text in response:

I'll try to fit you into my busy schedule.

I know I'm being unkind. After all, Gunner shouldn't have to stop his life just because he said he'd help me find my sister. But that doesn't mean that I don't wish he could move just a *little* faster.

Maybe he'll have some news to tell me when I see him later. A girl can hope, anyway.

After taking a shower and wandering aimlessly through the house for a while, I decide I need to get out of here and get some fresh air. I might as well spend the day exploring Tanner Springs on foot. I have no idea how far it is to the downtown area, but it's not like I have any pressing appointments later. Frankly the longer it takes me to get there and back, the less time I'll spend driving myself crazy turning in circles here at the house.

I slip on a pair of flip flops and head outside. Since I don't know much about the town except that we're on the east end of it, I decide just to head west. I walk slowly, to kill time, and eventually start seeing signs pointing me to the "business district." I turn left and continue walking in that direction. Pretty soon, I come up on a main street lined with shops on either side. The street covers several blocks, and my spirits lift just a little bit. If I take my time, I can probably waste a few hours wandering up and down exploring the shops.

I cross the street to the shady side, and start strolling. I pass by a thriving hardware store, a pharmacy, an ice cream place, a couple of beauty salons. Briefly, I consider going into one of the salons and getting a badly-needed trim, but I'm pretty sure I can't afford it

After about twenty minutes of wandering, I reach the end of the main drag. I cross the street and head back in the other direction. I go past a clothing store I can't afford, a pizza place that's not open for the day yet, and eventually stop in front of an inviting-looking coffee shop called the Golden Cup. I decide to spend a few dollars of my meager stash on a cup of something caffeinated. I skipped making coffee this morning, and sitting down for a few minutes sounds really inviting right now. Besides, after last night I could use something to cheer me up.

Inside, the atmosphere is warm and comforting. Dark wood and exposed brick walls give the shop a funky, homey vibe. About a third of the tables are occupied. Behind the counter, a strikingly pretty redhead is talking on a cell phone. When she sees me walk in, she flashes me a friendly smile and puts the phone down behind her.

"Hi, there. Welcome to the Golden Cup," she says.

"Hi," I smile back at her. I realize this is the first real interaction I've had with anyone in Tanner Springs except for

Gunner. The cashier at the grocery store doesn't count, because she didn't actually say words and seemed determined to avoid eye contact at all costs.

"I just finished decorating some cake bites," the redheaded woman says, pointing to a sample plate in front of her. "Feel free to help yourself."

"Thanks." I'm not about to turn down free sugar, especially not on my budget. The cake bites are about the size of a donut hole, and frosted in bright, happy colors. I select a blue one with sprinkles. Instead of popping the whole thing in my mouth, I bite it in half to make it last. The cake itself is moist and chocolatey, just sweet enough, and absolutely delicious.

"Oh, wow," I say when I've swallowed. "That's amazing!"

The redhead grins at me. "Thanks! I'm glad you like it. Some of the moms who come in here requested them for their little ones. So they can give them a treat that's not as big as a cookie or a muffin. Or as messy."

"I'm pretty sure these will be a big hit." I pop the other half of the cake bite into my mouth. *So* good.

"I'm Sydney, by the way," she says. "I don't think I've ever seen you in the shop before."

"I'm not from around here," I tell her. "I'm just in town for a few days. My name's Alix."

"Nice to meet you, Alix."

"Thank you." I cock my head. "Is this your shop?"

"Yes, it is," she says proudly. "I've been open about a year."

"It's really nice," I say sincerely. "Comfortable."

"Thanks!" She looks around the shop. "I took kind of a leap of faith opening it. I came here to Tanner Springs more or less on a whim. Luckily, everything seems to be working out."

"Oh, you're not from here either?" I ask. I feel a little weird asking, like I'm prying, but she doesn't seem to notice.

"Nope. I'm from Jersey," she says. "You?"

"Virginia. Lynchburg."

She nods. "Are you visiting family here?"

"Um… Sort of," I murmur evasively.

Sydney seems to sense my reticence, and doesn't push it. "Well. Tanner Springs is a pretty nice town, one you get to know it," she tells me. "Even though I had no idea what I was getting myself into when I came here, now I can't imagine living anywhere else." She glances up at the chalkboard with the list of drinks on it. "Do you know what you want, or should I stop babbling at you and give you a minute?"

I laugh. "I'll have a small mocha." The cake bite put me

in the mood for something sweet.

"You got it." Sydney tells me the price, and I hand her a bill. She gives me back my change. "Have a seat and I'll bring it out when it's ready."

I select a table by the window so I can watch the world go by. A minute later, Sydney appears. "Here you go."

"Thanks!" The cup she sets in front of me smells fantastic. Sydney leaves me alone with my drink, and I sip it slowly, enjoying it to the fullest. Like the cake bite, it's delicious. I imagine she gets a lot of repeat customers here.

Even though I've only traded sitting around in Gunner's house for sitting around in a coffee shop, just being around people and having a change of scenery makes me feel less anxious and frustrated about everything. I even manage to lose track of time a little bit. I'm enjoy watching people out the window as they walk by, and the customers who come in and out of Sydney's shop, when one customer walks in who almost makes me drop my coffee mug.

It's a tall, deeply tanned and muscular man with dark hair and eyes.

And he's wearing a Lords of Carnage vest.

And, as soon as Sydney sees him walk in, she lights up like a Christmas tree.

The man slips behind the counter and folds Sydney into his large embrace. He kisses her so deeply I feel like I'm spying and have to look away for a second. When he finally lets her go, she looks flustered but happy. She beams at him and says something in a low murmur that makes him throw back his head and roar with laughter.

It's all I can do not to just *stare* at the two of them. They look incredibly happy together. Any fool could see in an instant that they're deeply in love. My brain reels as I try to imagine how this dark, dangerous man let himself be tamed by the pretty coffee shop owner. But visibly, that's exactly what's happened. And even though you'd never guess it if you saw them separately, somehow they look sort of... *perfect* together. The yin to each other's yang.

The man leans down and says something in Sydney's ear, then kisses her again. My mind flashes to Gunner, and what happened the first night I spent at his house. Before I know it I'm blushing crimson, even though no one's even looking at me. The man with Sydney picks that exact moment to glance over toward me. Instantly I look away, and stare out the window, like I've just noticed something incredibly fascinating. A few seconds later, he slips back out from behind the counter and leaves, the shop bell sounding after him.

I don't know what possesses me to ask Sydney about the man. Her life is none of my business, after all. But she's been so open and friendly, I just can't help myself. I guess maybe I'm hoping to find out something — anything — about who Gunner is, and who the Lords of Carnage are.

When I approach the counter with my empty mug, she

thinks I'm just bringing it to her to bus my table. "Oh, thanks," she says, taking it from me. "Would you like a refill?"

"No, thanks. I should get going."

"Well, I hope you'll stop in again."

"I will," I promise, and then force myself to keep going. "Sydney," I begin, feeling awkward, "Can I ask you a question about… your boyfriend?" Good lord, if there was ever a guy that the word *boyfriend* didn't begin to describe, it's that one.

Her eyes widen for a second, and then she laughs. "His name is Gavin. Brick, to the MC."

MC. Oh, yeah. Motorcycle club.

"Oh." I take a breath. "Well, actually, the Lords of Carnage were kind of what I wanted to ask you about."

"Sure. I suppose you've seen them around town." She smiles kindly. "They might look dangerous, but they're actually pretty devoted to keeping Tanner Springs safe. You don't have anything to worry about from them."

"Oh, no, I'm… I mean, actually I know one of them. Gunner." I stumble a little over his name. It feels strange to be talking about him to someone else.

"You know Gunner?" She eyes me with a curious expression. "Really?"

"Yes. He's, uh, helping me look for someone." For some reason, I stop short of telling her I'm staying at his house. "My sister. She left home, and I just need to find her, and make sure she's okay."

Sydney shakes her head, looking amused. "Gunner, huh? Well, my goodness…"

"What?" I ask, a little afraid that she's going to tell me something I don't want to hear.

"Oh, nothing. Really." She gives me a reassuring grin. "Gunner's a really good guy, beneath the rough exterior. And I'll tell you one thing: if he says he's going to help you find your sister, you can bet he'll do it. You're in good hands with him." She winks conspiratorially. "Maybe in more ways than one."

Just then a customer comes in, and I'm left to ponder Sydney's words as she waves goodbye to me. It seems pretty obvious she meant it sexually. I'm guessing Gunner's got a reputation. I know from experience how good he is in bed. Maybe that's something all the other women know, too. My stomach rolls at the thought, my mouth tasting sour despite the delicious coffee drink I just finished.

Dammit, I *hate* that Gunner makes me feel like this. If it wasn't for Eden, I'd leave town right now and never look back. *Except that my car's in the club's shop now, that is.* Gunner was so mad at me last night he didn't even tell me what was wrong with it. A thin spike of worry jolts through me at the thought of having to pay a repair bill. But then I realize

Gunner probably won't let me pay for it anyway.

Far from being a relief, the thought of being even *further* in his debt is almost worse.

"*Why* didn't I just stay home in Lynchburg?" I murmur out loud to myself as I leave the coffee shop. This whole thing was a fool's errand. I'm never going to find Eden. I've lost my job, I'm running out of money, and I'm completely in over my head with a confusing, sexy man I wish I'd never met.

My phone vibrates in my pocket. I pull it out in irritation, sure it's Gunner demanding to know why I'm not at home.

But it's not Gunner.

It's *Eden*.

My heart begins to race as I read the short, blunt message. The brutal words that tell me in no uncertain terms to leave her the hell alone.

It's over, I think, choking back a deep sob that threatens to rip from my throat. *I was an idiot to think I was coming here to save her. I should have known she never wanted to see me again.*

Blindly, I start to stumble forward again, tears blurring my eyes. But then, just as I'm about to put the phone back in my pocket, something literally stops me in my tracks.

Behind me on the sidewalk, a teenage boy bumps into me. He swears in irritation, but I barely hear him.

I hold the phone up again stare at the screen.

All at once, I feel dizzy, like I'm going to pass out.

My hands start to tremble so badly I almost drop the thing as I find Gunner's number and press call. When he answers, I'm so upset I can barely speak.

"Gunner!" I choke out, "This is Alix! Please, come get me! Something's wrong!"

18
ALIX

Gunner tells me he's just getting back into town from his run with the club. It doesn't even take him fifteen minutes to get to the Golden Cup, but it feels like hours.

As soon as he ends the call, I start pacing back and forth in front of the coffee shop. My pulse is racing and I'm having trouble breathing. A few moments later, the door to the shop opens and Sydney comes out.

"Alix, are you okay?" she asks in a worried voice.

"No," I whisper. My heartbeat is pounding in my ears. "I don't think I am."

"Come back inside and sit down." A hand goes around my arm and pulls gently.

"I can't," I wheeze. "I have to wait out here for Gunner. He'll be here soon."

"Well, then, I'll wait out here with you," she says firmly. "You look like a ghost."

Thankfully, Sydney doesn't ask me to explain. She sits down on the curb with me, and tells me her customers can wait.

A few minutes later, Gunner comes flying up, and skids to a stop in front of us. He jumps off the bike and is in front of us in a second.

"I'm not sure what's wrong," Sydney tells him. "She looks sick, but she says she's not."

"I know," he says. "Thanks for taking care of her." He turns to me. "You okay to ride?"

I nod. "Yes," I manage to say.

"Okay, then. Let's go. I'm taking you to the clubhouse."

* * *

"This is the text I got from her phone."

I pull out my cell and show Gunner and a thin, lanky man he calls Tweak. We're at the Lords of Carnage clubhouse, sitting in a small, sparse room with a few computer monitors on a long desk in front of us.

Gunner takes the phone and peers at it, then passes it to the other man.

"At first, I thought it was her. I was so excited that she'd texted me, and then so crushed by what she said, that I didn't look very closely." I swallow and try to push down the panic. "But then I noticed how she spelled my name."

"A-l-e-x," Tweak reads.

"My name's spelled with an 'i'," I tell him. "Eden would never have made that mistake. This can't be her."

Gunner takes the phone back from him and reads the entire text out loud.

"Alex, I don't want to see you. Go back to Lynchburg and leave me the hell alone."

He frowns at me. "'Go *back* to Lynchburg'?"

I nod. "I know." I turn to Tweak. "Yesterday, I did something stupid and went to the Smiling Skull myself," I explain. "Gonzalo wasn't there. But maybe someone there heard me asking about him, and warned him someone was looking for him. Maybe he put two and two together."

Tweak nods. "That makes sense."

"Shit," Gunner rasps. All the anger he didn't let out at me last night comes rushing to the surface. "Goddamnit, Alix. I told you to let me take care of this! If Gonzalo's figured out you're still here sniffing around —"

"I know!" I say, cutting him off. "I know. And I'm sorry, Gunner. I really am. I was an idiot." I glance back down at the phone. "And this is bad. But maybe it's good, too. It tells us *something*. Maybe Eden really does need help. And maybe this tells us she really is with Gonzalo!"

"She's right," Tweak says to Gunner. "It's better than nothing."

Gunner's jaw clenches angrily. He looks at Tweak. "Keep looking for Gonzalo's address. I need to bring Alix up to speed on some shit."

"One more thing," Tweak asks me. "You got a picture of your sister?"

I take my phone back from Gunner and flip through my photos until I find one. I hold it out to show them. Eden's basically a brunette version of me, with light chestnut hair, darker brows, and the same wide, light brown eyes that we got from our mom. In this picture, a coy, flirtatious smile graces her features, making her look like she's issuing a challenge to whoever took the photo.

Tweak whistles when he sees it. "She's a knockout."

Gunner flashes him a warning look.

"Yes," I say softly. "She is."

Tweak has me send the photo to him and Gunner. Then Gunner and I leave to let him work, and go back down the long narrow hallway back toward where we came in.

The large main room we enter is deserted. Gunner walks over to a long bar counter off to one side and leans an elbow on it. "I found out Gonzalo is based out of a town called Red Hawk," he says without preamble. "Red Hawk's about twenty minutes south of the Smiling Skull. The town's in territory occupied by another MC, called the Death Devils." As I digest this information, he continues. "Tweak's looking for where Gonzalo lives right now. After that, he'll work on getting the location of where his crew operates out of."

"Operates? What do you mean?"

For a few seconds, Gunner doesn't respond. "We're pretty sure they're involved in drug dealing. Mostly heroin."

Shit. Is Eden mixed up in all that? I know she used to smoke a lot of pot in high school, and I wouldn't be surprised if she's tried other stuff, too, but *heroin*? It's almost impossible for me to imagine her taking drugs that hard. But I have to admit to myself I might not know my sister nearly as well as I hope I do.

I open my mouth to ask another question, but just then the front door slams open with a loud bang. Male laughter reaches my ears. I swivel around to see half a dozen Lords of Carnage striding in. All of them are big, tattooed, and dangerous-looking.

"Gun!" one yells with a lewd chuckle. "You brought me a present? Hell, it ain't even my birthday!"

"Shut it, Sarge," Gunner growls. He leans close. "Stay

close to me," he tells me. "At least at first. None of the men will try anything once they know you're with me. But until then, you're better off not wandering."

For the first time since I hopped on his bike to come here, it occurs to me that place could be just as dangerous as the Smiling Skull. Maybe more dangerous. Even though I'm with someone I'm pretty sure will protect me, a wave of fear squeezes my lungs until it's a little hard to breathe.

At the sound of the men entering, a few women filter in from other rooms in the clubhouse, chattering excitedly. Most of the them look like plastic blow-up dolls, made up like porn stars with the clothes to match. Even so, the men are looking at me with open curiosity, and some with unconcealed lust. A few of them give me leers that I'd be shrinking from if Gunner wasn't here to protect me. The women examine me with expressions ranging from indifference to contempt.

"This is Alix," Gunner calls in a loud voice. "She's with me. Understood?"

Another male voice calls out, "Did you bring enough to share with the rest of the class?" Raucous laughter erupts.

Gunner leans toward me. "It's okay. The men know you're off limits now."

I'm not sure I believe him, but at this point I don't have much choice. As we stand there, three of the Lords walk toward us. My eyes widen as I recognize two of them.

"Alix," Gunner growls. "This is Angel, Thorn, and Brick."

"Hi," I say in a small voice, blushing in spite of myself.

"Welcome to our castle, little lady," the one called Thorn says with a wink and a roguish grin. "Remember me?"

"I do," I smile shyly at him. "You were at the Smiling Skull that night."

"I was," he nods. "Glad to see you've recovered. That was a bad business."

"And actually, I know you, too," I say, turning to Brick. At his surprised look, I continue. "I was just at the Golden Cup coffee shop. You came in to talk to Sydney."

Brick frowns, and then his eyebrows raise in recognition. "You were sitting over by the window."

"Yes!"

He nods. "Huh. Small world. That your first time in the shop?"

"Uh-huh. Sydney was really nice to me."

"Good to hear."

I can't believe I'm standing here just talking to these outlaw bikers like I would be to any other normal person. The strangeness of almost everything that's happened to me in the last few days comes telescoping up at me suddenly, and

I have to fight the urge to start laughing half-hysterically. Gunner is looking back and forth from me to Brick, like he can hardly believe it either.

Just then, something across the room catches his eye. I follow his gaze and see Tweak raising a finger at us. Leaning down, Gunner murmurs in my ear. "I know I said to stay next to me, but you're good now. I need to talk to Tweak for a second. I'll be right back."

I watch Gunner walk off. Brick takes his leave of us, too, and goes over to join another small group of men. Beside me, Thorn speaks up.

"So, you've decided to stay and experience the bustling metropolis that is Tanner Springs," he says, giving me another wink.

"For now. It's a little smaller than I'm used to," I admit. "But actually, I kind of like it so far."

"Are yeh staying here in town, then?" Thorn asks.

"Yes." I hesitate for a second. "Actually, I'm staying at Gunner's place for now. In his guest room," I add quickly.

Thorn smirks like he doesn't believe me for a second. "Uh-huh. Funny, that. Gunner doesn't often have 'guests'."

"He's helping me try and find my sister," I say, ignoring the flush that heats my cheeks. "That's who I was looking for that night at the Smiling Skull."

Thorn nods sagely. "I see. No luck so far, then?"

"Not yet."

"Well." Thorn raises a bottle of beer and takes a swig. "If Gunner says he'll find her for you, he will. You can count on that. Gunner's a man of his word."

Sydney said the same thing when I was in her shop. But somehow coming from one of his club brothers makes my heart leap. "You really think so?"

"I do." He lifts his chin toward Gunner and Tweak in the corner. "He'll do what he says he will. That's a promise. And if he needs the club to help him, we're there."

My eyes unexpectedly fill with tears, and I have to look away and blink several times to hold them back. For the first time since I left Virginia, I actually feel almost hopeful.

"Here, and I've been talking your ear off all this time," Thorn says cheerfully, "And no one's offered you anything to drink. Would you like a beer?"

"Actually, yes," I say thankfully.

He goes behind the bar to grab two cold bottles. "Our normal bartender's not due in until a bit later," Thorn tells me. "So I'm at your service."

I can't help but laugh at being waited on by a man who's almost twice my size. Thorn nods approvingly. "There's her smile," he says. Twisting off the cap, he hands the beer to me.

"And this will make you feel even better."

"I hope so," I say as I raise it to him and take a drink. "The last few days have been kind of tough."

Thorn stays and chats with me flirtatiously, which should make me nervous but somehow doesn't. By about halfway through my beer, I'm laughing uproariously at something he's said, which seems to only spur him on.

Suddenly, Gunner's there, standing next to me and eyeing Thorn with an expression I don't quite understand, but which makes Thorn burst into loud laughter.

"Don't worry, brother, ye've already marked yer territory," he says in a teasing tone. "Seemed like the lady could use some cheering up, though, so I thought I'd oblige."

"Yeah. Well, go *oblige* somewhere else," Gunner warns in a tone I've never heard from him before. Thorn snorts and gives me a final wink, then moves away.

"Why were you being so rude to him?" I snap at Gunner as he pulls up a stool next to me. "He was just being nice."

"Yeah," Gunner mutters. "I've seen his 'nice.' That ain't it."

If I didn't know better, I'd think Gunner was actually *jealous*. "Are you saying he was trying to make some sort of *move* on me?" I ask, half-angry. "I thought you said no one would try anything if you told them not to."

"Thorn can't help himself." Gunner rolls his eyes and shakes his head. "He knows all he has to do is open his mouth and panties drop as soon as women hear the Irish accent."

"So, you're saying what?" I ask, my voice rising with my anger. "That I have no self-control? That I just automatically *drop my panties* whenever a guy wants me to?"

"Goddamnit, that's not what I'm saying at all," he grunts in exasperation. "Look. Subject closed."

"No," I spit back, my chin jutting out. "Subject open. Just what *are* you trying to say, then?"

Gunner's eyes turn dark and stormy. "Right now, I'm trying to say you're being a colossal pain in the ass."

What the hell? Gunner's never been like this with me. I don't even understand why he's so angry with me. It *can't* be because he's jealous of Thorn. Can it?

The idea that maybe he *is* jealous is enough to give me a little thrill. But unfortunately, I'm mad enough at what a jackass he's being that anger overrides everything else.

"You know what, Gunner?" I hiss. "I appreciate that you are trying to help me find my sister. But after me waiting by myself for the better part of *two solid days* in your house with nothing to do, while you mostly ignore me, *now* you're pissed that I'm actually having a conversation with someone else?" I plant my fists on my hips and square my stance. "I can talk to whomever I want, thank you very much. And just because you think you're being some kind of hero protector doesn't mean you get to control what I do and don't do."

"Little girl, you don't know what the hell you're talking about," he growls.

"Don't give me that," I scoff. "You know damn well you're trying to control me."

"I ain't trying a damn thing," he half-roars. "I'm doing. It's about time you learn that I'm already in control, darlin'." Gunner grabs me roughly by the arm and pulls me toward a staircase leading to the second floor. "And two minutes from now, you'll never doubt that again."

19
GUNNER

Shit. As hard as I've tried to keep my dick in my pants and my hands off Alix for the last couple of days, seeing the fire of challenge in her eyes just now pretty much undoes me.

I kept telling myself that even though Alix seems to have taken up permanent residence in my head, one willing pussy is just as good as another. And God knows, there's plenty of willing pussy around me at the clubhouse.

But then I see that son of a bitch Thorn making her laugh. She looks at him with a carefree, unguarded expression I've never seen on her face before. And I see red. Blood fucking red. If Thorn wasn't my brother, I'd pound his ass into the goddamn ground.

And then the next thing I know, I'm pulling Alix upstairs with me, with her bitching the whole goddamn way.

Alix is off limits. To everyone but me.

"How dare you!" she snarls when I've pushed her inside my apartment and shut the door. "You can barely be bothered to give me the time of day for the last *two days*! And now that someone in your club at least takes a moment to try to make me feel a little comfortable here, instead of just *ignoring* me, you suddenly give a shit?" She flings her hands in the air in exasperation. "That's not how it works, Gunner."

In spite of everything, I have to laugh. "That's what you think is happening? I've been *ignoring* you?"

"What the hell else would you call it then?" she challenges. "Leaving me alone in your house to just twiddle my damn thumbs all day?"

I pull her roughly against me. I can tell by the way she draws in a sharp breath that she can feel how hard I already am for her.

Alix stares up at me with wide, dark eyes. Her lips part. She draws in a sharp breath.

She knows what's coming as well as I do.

"I haven't been ignoring you darlin'," I growl, leaning down and nipping the sensitive lobe of her ear. She moans and involuntarily presses herself against me. "I've been stayin' away from you for your own good. But that ends now. You've pushed me to the limit, Alix, and it's time I showed you who's boss."

I bring my hand to the back of her head and hold it as I kiss that smart mouth of hers. My tongue slides between her lips and she moans again, her hips moving against my hard length. *Sweet Jesus*, I can hardly stop myself from just tearing off her clothes and taking her just like that. It's barely been two days but it feels like a goddamn eternity. Especially because I *know* what she feels like, I *know* how hard I'm gonna come, and I can hardly wait for it.

But I *will* wait for it. Because she needs to know who's in control. And for that, she's gotta beg me for it.

"Strip. I want you naked. Now."

For a second, I think she's gonna argue with me. But then I see the look in her eyes, and I know. She's thinking about the last time we fucked, too. She wants it. She'll do anything I tell her to, because she knows how good it's gonna feel.

Slowly, she reaches up and slides her little T-shirt up her ribcage, past her full breasts, and over her neck. She tosses it to the floor, her eyes never leaving mine. Then, her breath shallow and fast, she reaches up and shimmies out of her bra. Her tits fall, round and heavy, the nipples already tight and waiting for me. She unbuttons her jeans and starts to push the waistband over her hips.

"Leave the panties," I tell her. She does as she's told, to my satisfaction.

Then she's standing there, a fucking vision in front of me. I can tell she's already wet as hell for me.

It should be a sin to be that goddamn sexy.

"On your knees," I command.

Almost instantly, she's down on the ground, looking up at me with lustful, willing eyes. Fuck, she looks *hungry* for my cock. It's gonna take all the self-control I can muster to hold myself back.

I yank off my shirt and kick off my jeans. Then I stand in front of her for a second, my dick throbbing in anticipation. She moves forward just a little, but then stops and waits for me to tell her what to do. *Good girl.*

"You fucking love this," I tell her. "Don't you? You love being told what to do."

Her face flushes pink. She looks down and bites her lip. "Yes," she admits in a whisper.

I chuckle low in my throat. I can tell she's surprised, herself. She's used to being the responsible one. The one who takes care of her dying mother. The one whose job it is to rescue her wayward sister. Having someone else take charge is new to her. And she likes it.

Being controlled in the bedroom turns her on more than she wants to admit.

"Suck me," I say bluntly.

A sexy little whimper sounds deep in her throat as she moves forward and takes my shaft in her hand. She wraps her lips around the head of my cock, and I draw in a breath and hiss at how good it feels. Jesus *Christ*, her tongue slides around the ridge underneath the head, and then she starts to suck, pulling about half my length into her mouth and as far back as she can go. I go rigid and let myself thrust as little as possible, half-crazy from the pleasure but absolutely committed to not letting myself come — partly because I'm afraid I'll fucking drown her, and partly because when I *do* come, it's gonna be with me deep inside that fucking luscious pussy of hers.

Alix is getting worked up now, moaning softly as she sucks and bobs, the thrum of her voice vibrating against my shaft. Goddamn, one of these days, I'm gonna let go like this, and my head might just explode when I do. But for now I have to stop her. I pull away suddenly, grabbing her hair in my hand as gently as I'm able to.

"That's enough, darlin'," I mutter. Letting go of her hair, I reach down and take her hand, helping her up. "Bed," I order, nodding my head in the direction I want her to go. She gives a little moue of protest, but does what I say before I can reprimand her.

She lies down on the bed, pressing her legs shyly together. Her breasts are heaving now, the nipples taut and ready for me. I kneel down beside her and pull her knees apart, chuckling low in my throat when I see how soaking wet her panties are.

"Fuck," I rasp. "You're ready as hell for me, aren't you, baby girl?"

She flushes a darker shade of pink at my words, but doesn't look away when my eyes lock on hers.

"Tell me, darlin'," I insist.

"Yes," she admits in a whisper.

I reach between her legs and slide the thin fabric aside with a finger, just grazing the soft skin of her swollen lips as I do. Alix throws back her head and gasps, arching her hips toward me. Fuck, she's so ready. Suddenly, I can't wait a second longer to taste her. I push her knees apart and position myself between them. Her thighs tense in anticipation. I open my mouth and take a long, slow lap at her pussy. Alix gasps again, her thighs falling open even further. I pull her hips roughly toward me and swipe at her again, reveling in how sweet she tastes, how fucking delicious she is. She cries out and angles her hips to meet my tongue. I hear rather than see her hands as they take hold of the bedspread and clench as she tries to find purchase.

Fuck, yes.

I start to lick her just a little faster, just a little harder, listening to her moans and cries get louder and more desperate. Whenever she starts to get close, I back off, just enough, and then start building again, pushing her higher and higher, then taking it away.

"Gunner," she moans. "Please, make me come. Let me come."

"I decide when you come, baby girl. And it's not yet."

I tease her more, my cock so hard it feels like I'm gonna go off like a goddamn time bomb. I could come like this, without even touching myself, I'm so turned on by how fucking delicious she is and how much she wants this. Pretty soon Alix is dangerously close, a hair trigger, and I know exactly how and where to lick her to push her over the edge. Her head begins to thrash against the mattress, her breathing fast and shallow, her body tense like a rubber band.

"Your pussy tastes so goddamn good. Tell me what you want, baby."

"Oh, God! Gunner, *please*!" she begs.

Then, I slide my tongue long and slow over her clit — *right* where I know she needs it — and bury it deep in her pussy as she screams and bucks like a slingshot. Her whole body jolts at once, convulsing in the throes of an orgasm so intense that I can almost feel every one of her muscles contracting. I keep licking and suckling at her nub as she shakes and quivers under my tongue. It's easily the hottest goddamn thing I've ever seen, felt, or heard in my entire goddamn life.

Alix is still shuddering when I raise myself up and flip her over so she's on her hands and knees. I rip her panties off her with my bare hands and toss the remnants on the floor. Somehow, I remember to slip on a condom before I kneel between her legs and sink myself deep inside her.

"Jesus fucking Christ," I groan. I freeze for a second, half afraid I'll come before I even get started. After a moment, I manage to calm myself down enough to draw out slowly and then slide back in.

"Oh, God, yes," Alix moans. Her pussy clenches around my cock.

My hands grip her hips tightly. Fuck, I already knew how good she felt from the first time but it's *still* a surprise.

"Fuck me," she whispers. Her hips arch against me, pulling me in deeper.

That's all it takes. With one hand, I reach around, sliding a finger around her slick clit. I brace myself against her with the other hand and begin thrusting, slow at first, but before long faster and faster. Alix's muscles pulse around my cock, our bodies finding a rhythm that pulls us both in. Then I'm right there, on the edge, and it's only a matter of seconds before…

"Gunner!" Alix cries out again, and begins to shake as a second orgasm rips through her. I thrust again, once, twice, and then I release myself deep inside her, coming so hard I worry for a second that the condom will break. I think I yell, but I can't be sure of anything except this, and her, and how good this feels, and then I'm lying down, still inside her, pulling her against me as the two of us ride out the wave.

If I thought fucking her again would get Alix Cousins out of my system, I was dead fucking wrong.

I'm kissing her deeply, her head tilted back to meet my mouth, when there's a loud bang on the door. In my arms, Alix jumps.

"What the fuck is it?" I roar, holding her fast so she won't spring up off the bed.

"Gun! Sorry to interrupt your recreational activities," Thorn calls out, his tone amused.

Son of a bitch. "What the fuck do you want, Thorn?" I ask in a warning voice.

"Tweak sent me up to get you. He's got an address."

20
ALIX

I'm shaky and unsteady on my feet as Gunner helps me up off the bed. I'm already sore between my legs, and I know I'm going to be even more sore later. But somehow, I'm *glad* to be sore. It feels good to take a physical memory with me of what just happened between us.

"There's a bathroom through that door." Gunner points with one hand, pulling off the condom with the other. "Go ahead and get cleaned up. We should go downstairs and find out what Tweak's got."

I do as he says, shutting the bathroom door behind me carefully. My head is still kind of reeling from what just happened. Being around Gunner makes me feel like I never quite know what's going on, or what's going to happen next. One minute, I think he's ignoring me and only helping me out of some sense of obligation. The next, he's got his tongue between my legs and driving me out of my mind. Just now, when he came inside me… it felt so good I almost cried. It was even more intense than the first time with him.

God help me, it's *never* felt like this before, with any man. It's so good that I almost wish it had never happened. Because I know this isn't a long-term thing. It's basically just a one-night stand, artificially prolonged because for some reason Gunner's agreed to help me find my sister.

And even though I don't know him that well, everyone says he's a man of his word. Which means I know he won't rest until we've located Eden.

But I hope it also means that he won't pretend that this… *thing* between us isn't something serious.

I'm not stupid. I know it's just sex.

But even though I know it's ridiculous of me, I can already tell that when it's all over, I'm going to suffer.

Somehow, Gunner has sort of gotten to me. Being with him makes me wish for things I can't have. I can't help but wish that he felt the same way.

If it wasn't for the fact that I can't find Eden by myself, I'd run away from this. Before I get hurt even more than I know I already will be when this is over.

But I can't run until I know she's safe. Even though every day I stay in Tanner Springs, I run the risk of my heart being broken just a little more.

I splash some cold water over my face, and finger-comb the just-fucked look out of my hair. It doesn't help all that much. When I emerge from the bathroom, Gunner's already dressed, and my clothes are in a small pile on the bed. Wordlessly, I start pulling them on, feeling awkward that I'm still naked and he isn't.

Once I'm finished, he strides to the door and holds it open for me. I almost laugh at the unexpectedly chivalrous move, and he must see my lips quirk up.

"What?" he asks.

"Nothing," I murmur. "Just… this is a pretty far cry from the way we came in."

Gunner catches me around the waist as I walk through. "I'm not a total caveman," he growls into my hair. Even though he just made me come *twice*, I'm instantly wet for him.

"I wouldn't say *that*," I say breathily, teasing him. Laughter rumbles up from deep in his throat.

"Watch it, darlin'." He pulls me against him, and somehow he's hard *again*. "Or I may just have to live up to your filthy expectations of me."

We walk downstairs, him following behind me. Down below, a few of the men look up and start hooting and catcalling. I realize they must have heard us — me, especially — and I have to fight the urge to run back into the apartment and hide. I guess we were a little louder than I thought.

"Ignore those idiots," Gunner grunts, reading my thoughts. "Come on, let's go back and find Tweak."

He leads me to the back of the bar and into the small room with the computer monitors where we were before.

"You got us an address?" Gunner asks him without preamble.

"Yeah." Tweak gestures toward the middle screen, which shows a Google Earth aerial view of a small, squarish house with a large, cluttered yard on what appears to be a small rural county road. "That's where Gonzalo lives, I'm pretty sure. It's about fifteen minutes outside of Red Hawk."

Tweak tells Gunner the address, which he doesn't bother to write down. "Okay," Gunner says. "I'm gonna go talk to Rock about taking a few of the brothers out there."

"You told the prez about any of this yet?" Tweak asks.

"No. But Angel knows. He'll back me up."

Tweak nods. "You want me to come with you guys?"

"Not yet. I need you here. Keep digging up intel, in case this ends up being a dead end. We still need to find where Gonzalo's crew does their business."

"Yup," Tweak responds, and turns back to his computer screens.

Just like that, the conversation's over, and I'm practically running to keep up with Gunner as he strides back out into the bar area.

"I want to come with you," I pant.

Gunner turns on his heel and practically glares at me.

"Abso-fucking-lutely not," he growls. "It's too dangerous."

"Dammit, Gunner!" I practically wail. "I've been sitting around on my hands for days now. I can't just do nothing while you go out and get her."

"Yes you goddamn can," he retorts. "You realize how dangerous this is? If you go with us, we'll have to protect you. Which means less energy and focus on protecting and rescuing your sister, if she's there. You get that?"

"But—"

"No fucking buts," he cuts me off. "If you want her to be safe, you need to stay out of it, and wait here."

Thorn appears at my side. "He's right, darlin'. Let the Lords handle this for now. It's the best chance you have to get your sister back."

Gunner glares at Thorn but says nothing. I sigh loudly and admit defeat. "Fine," I spit out. "So, what? I just stay here?"

"Didn't you say you'd met Sydney?" Thorn asks. "Why don't we ask Brick to call her? She can come here to the clubhouse and keep you company while we're gone."

I smile at Thorn gratefully and look at Gunner. "Good idea," he says grudgingly.

"'Course it is," Thorn grins, a roguish twinkle in his eye. "As are all my ideas."

"Thorn, you're coming with me to find Gonzalo," Gunner glowers, and stomps off.

"I do believe he's taking me along to keep an eye on me." Thorn winks at me.

I roll my eyes. "That's ridiculous."

"Hardly," Thorn laughs. "If I had a woman that looked like you, I'd get me out of the picture, too."

I open my mouth to protest, but Thorn's already sauntering over to Brick. They speak a few words, then Brick looks over at me, nods, and pulls out his phone. I guess Sydney will be coming to keep me company after all.

* * *

It only takes about ten minutes for Gunner to assemble a group of four other men, including Thorn, a man named

Beast who I recognize from the Smiling Skull, and two others named Hawk and Bullet. The five of them take off, leaving me alone to kill time until Sydney arrives. I wander over to the bar, where a woman who introduces herself as Jewel is now behind the counter. She serves me the club soda that I ask for, and tells me to let her know if I need anything.

Spying a cluster of low, comfortable couches, I make my way over to them and sit down with my drink to wait.

I'm absently flipping through some random social media posts, nursing my club soda, when a clacking of approaching heels makes me look up. A tall strawberry blond in a skin-tight black miniskirt and a hot pink tank top with a Harley logo is gazing down at me, her pink lips contorted into a slight sneer.

"You're wasting your time, missy," she scoffs.

Missy? My dislike of her is instant, but I fight to keep it off my face. "Excuse me?"

"I don't know what sob story you've given to Gunner to make him feel sorry for you," she continues, putting one fist on her hip, "But don't get any stupid ideas. You're not his type."

Is this seriously happening right now? "Not his type?" I say in disbelief. "What the hell are you talking about?"

"You think because he's paying you a little attention right now, that he's not gonna just drop you like a hot potato once he's had his fun?" She snorts softly. "Sorry to tell you,

Gunner ain't gonna give you his class ring. He ain't gonna take you to the prom, and whatever little white picket fence future you're imagining isn't gonna happen. You may as well know the truth from the get-go."

"Excuse me," I say coldly, "but my life and whatever *is* or *is not* happening between Gunner and me is none of your business."

The woman throws back her head and laughs uproariously. "Oh, Jesus Christ, you *do* think he's gonna put a ring on it, don't you?" She shakes her head at me, pity dripping from her voice. "Sorry, sweetheart. He just ain't that into you."

"How the fuck would you know anything about it one way or another?" I spit back, and inwardly wince that I'm letting her get to me.

She shoots me an ugly smirk. "Because he's been fucking me every chance he gets. For months. And I can do things to him that a little priss like you would never know how to do in a million years."

My stomach jumps unpleasantly in my gut. Is she telling the truth? Is Gunner fucking this… *whorebag* at the same time that he's been sleeping with me? Something in my face must register my dismay, because the bitch laughs again, crossing her arms over her surgically-enhanced tits with a mocking smile.

Oh, *hell* no. I am not giving her the satisfaction of scoring a point off me. I am *done* with this conversation.

"Look," I bite out, getting to my feet. With her in stilettos that are at least three inches high, she's got a good six inches over me, but I don't care — my blood is starting to boil.

"I don't know what the fuck your problem is. But I'll tell you this. If Gunner's fucking *me*, that clearly means he's not getting what he needs from *you*. Which, you know, I can understand." I take a long, slow look at her from the ground up, obviously judging her 'assets'. "Cheap whores like you are a dime a dozen. Maybe Gunner just wanted something a little less... common."

The whore's face turns from smug to furious in a heartbeat. "You fucking bitch!" she screams, turning scarlet with rage. She takes a step forward, raising her hands like she's getting ready to claw my eyes out with her porn nails. I move into a crouch, scared but determined to give as good as I get.

Just as she starts to launch herself at me, though, a set of masculine hands grab her by the upper arms and roughly pull her back.

"Jesus fucking Christ, Heather," rumbles Brick. "What the fuck is wrong with you?"

"This *bitch* insulted me!" she yells, pulling against Brick's steely grip to try to get herself loose. It's useless, though — it's almost like a stone statue has hold of her because Brick is not budging.

"Calm the fuck down!" he roars back, holding her fast.

"Let me *go*!" she screams as she continues to struggle.

"For fuck's sake," Brick mutters in a disgusted voice. "Heather!" He brings her closer until she is mere inches from him, getting in her face until she blanches and finally calms down a little. "You knock this *shit* off! Alix is here because Gunner wants her to be." He nods toward me. "You say another word to her — *one more word* — you are out of here. For good. You hear me?"

The bitch yanks her arm back defiantly just as Brick lets go, which causes her to stumble back on her heels. She flies backwards and flops ungracefully down on the low overstuffed couch, her legs splaying out wildly. In spite of myself, I actually start laughing. It's a welcome relief from the tension and anger I was feeling just moments ago.

Behind me, another female voice starts laughing as well. I turn around to see Sydney standing there.

"Hey, girl!" she greets me.

"Hey!" I grin, thrilled to see a friendly face. "I didn't see you there."

"I just got here." She glances down dismissively at the prone figure on the couch. "I see you've met Heather," she says with disgust.

"Yeah," I nod, glancing back as well. "I've had the dubious pleasure."

From the couch, Heather mutters something I can't quite hear, but that doesn't exactly sound friendly.

"Dubious is right. Come on," Sydney says, rolling her eyes. "Let's go over to the bar and hang out with Jewel for a while. The club *whores*" — she calls out the word after Heather for emphasis — "won't bother you any more now."

21
GUNNER

Hawk, Beast, and I head out on our bikes. Thorn and Bullet follow in one of the club's pickups, an F-150 with a hard top over the cab. The pickup's in case we end up having to take a hostage with us on the way back. Or a body.

We ride east for almost two hours, toward the address Tweak gave me. We end up at a small, ramshackle farmhouse out in the middle of Bumfuck, Egypt. I signal to Thorn and Bullet to hang back and park the pickup out of sight further up the road. They move silently through the thicket of trees surrounding the house's yard, coming up around the other side to watch the back. Hawk, Beast, and I park the bikes halfway up the driveway between the house and the road. Reflexively, I make sure my pistol's securely tucked into the waistband of my jeans. When I give Hawk and Beast the nod, we and start walking up the gravel drive to the farmhouse.

In the distance, I can hear the bark of a dog. There's an

old, dusty Chevy Impala parked off to the side of the house that doesn't look like it's been used in a while. It's impossible to tell whether anyone's home.

We move closer slowly, hands at the ready, scanning the house and yard for any signs of movement. In my peripheral vision, I just barely see what I think is a figure moving past one of the front windows.

"Hello?" Thorn calls out. "Anybody home?"

From inside, I just make out a low thud. Then, a second later, a loud crack pierces the silence, followed by a whiz by my right ear.

"Gun!" I roar.

I drop to the ground. Off to my right I see Hawk and Beast do the same. I pull myself over behind an old, disused clawfoot bathtub planter filled with dirt, the only cover close to me. A few yards away, Hawk rolls behind the trunk of a tree.

Off in the distance, I see Bullet running in a low crouch toward the back of the house.

Another bullet whizzes past me. I raise my head up enough over the clawfoot to take aim. I squeeze the trigger and instantly duck back down, just in time to hear the smashing glass as the front picture window of the house shatters from the bullet.

"God damnit!" an angry male voice yells.

"The next one goes through your skull!" I yell back.

For a few seconds, there's silence.

"You cops?" a craggy, female smoker's voice calls out.

"No, we're not fucking cops!" Beast shouts in disgust. "For fuck's sake!"

In back, there's the sound of splintering wood as either Thorn or Bullet kicks the door in. After a few moments of commotion inside, and another gunshot, Thorn yells to us: "We got 'em! It's all clear!"

Cautiously, Hawk and Beast emerge from their covers, and we approach the house. Just as we get to the porch, Thorn opens the front door.

"Feckin' gobshite meth heads," he spits in disgust.

Hawk stays out on the porch to watch for cars. Beast and I enter the house.

Inside, it smells vaguely of piss and old food. The place is a fucking sty, the walls greasy and stained. Old, ratty furniture looks like it was fished out of a dumpster. Bullet is training his pistol on two emaciated people with their hands up: a man and a woman whose drug addled features could place them anywhere on the age spectrum from mid-thirties to mid-fifties. On the floor is a shotgun.

"Check the rest of the house," I tell Thorn and Beast. They move off down the hallway, pistols drawn.

"Who the fuck are you?" the man risks the question.

"None of your fucking business," I tell him. "Where's Gonzalo?"

"Who wants to know?" the woman sneers, revealing uneven and yellowed teeth.

"My fucking Glock 27," Bullet growls, indicating the pistol that's trained on them. "You're gonna want to give him an answer, right goddamn now."

"Gonzalo ain't here," the man says.

"He live here?" I ask.

"Sometimes. He ain't been here for a coupla weeks."

"He have a bedroom here?"

"Yeah. Upstairs, the last one on the right. The blue one."

Thorn and Beast come back downstairs. I ask him if he found anything useful in the blue bedroom.

"Nah. Just some weed and pills. Couple of spare mags but no guns. Must have 'em with him."

"Whatchu lookin' for anyway?" the woman asks. "He got something of yours?"

"Something like that." I take a step forward and fix her eyes with mine. "You know where he is?"

The woman snorts. "He don't tell me anything. His own mother. He just comes and goes as he pleases."

"You sure about that?" I ask. Reaching into the breast pocket of my cut, I pull out a few bills and hold them up. "A hundred dollars would buy a hell of a lot of whatever the two of you are smoking."

"Maybe he's over to Maverick's," the suddenly-helpful man offers as he eyes the money. "Strip club, out on the other side of town."

"Darren, goddamnit!" the woman spits out.

"I know where it is," I tell him.

"He goes there pretty often. Knows the owner."

"That's pretty damn vague," I say, handing him a bill. "Here's a twenty." I nod to my brothers. "Okay, I think we're done here." I pick up the shotgun on the floor. The man starts to protest.

"I'll leave it out by the side of the road," I say, cutting him off. "Can't have you shooting at us as we leave, now can we?"

We have the two of them lie down on the ground, and back out the door to make sure they're following instructions to stay put until we're gone.

"You think they're telling us the truth about not knowing where he is?" I ask Bullet as we walk back out to the vehicles.

"Maybe." He raises a hand and rubbed it across his clean-shaven skull. Bullet got patched into the club about a year ago, but he's as solid and tough as they come. He's one of the first men I'd want with me in any dangerous situation.

Beast comes up beside us. "His room didn't look like he'd been there for a while. Lots of undisturbed dust on shit."

"Thank God for shitty meth head housekeeping," I chuckle.

"What do we do now?" Bullet asks.

"Go out to Maverick's," I say. "Maybe we'll get lucky and he'll be there. If not, we still get to have fun looking around."

* * *

At two o'clock in the afternoon at a strip club, there isn't a whole hell of a lot going on. A couple of boozers at the bar. A lone woman working the pole in a stripper version of a schoolgirl uniform. Three other scantily clad women sitting around at a back table, looking like they're waiting for some paying customers to arrive. They perk up when we come in, but lose interest when it becomes clear we aren't here for recreation.

I walk up to the bar and lean on the counter. The bartender spots me and ambles over.

"Can I help you gentlemen?" he asks.

"I need to see the owner. He around?"

"Yeah. He's in the back. Hold on."

The bartender looks like he's not quite sure about leaving us alone, but he does it anyway, giving us one final glance before he heads down the hall. A minute or so later he returns, followed by a middle-aged guy in a black shirt and jean jacket. He's wearing an obvious hairpiece styled like he got it off a seventies-era porn actor.

The man walks up to the five of us, his face a suspicious frown. "You wanted to see me?"

"Yeah." I take a step forward. "I'm looking for Gonzalo Medina. Somebody told me you're a buddy of his."

"Who wants to know?" he asks, his chin jutting forward.

I cut a sideways glance at Thorn and the others. I don't have time for bullshit. "Let's take this outside."

"I ain't goin' outside," the guy says obstinately, squaring his shoulders.

"I suggest that you are," I tell him. "Unless you want this to get ugly in front of your paying customers." He opens his mouth to resist, but I cut him off. "You aren't in any danger, as long as you do what we say. We just have a couple of questions."

Not waiting for an answer, I stride to the door and push it open. When I get to the parking lot and turn around, I see he's decided to comply. The other Lords surround him as soon as he's through the door, to make sure he doesn't try to make a run for it or something equally stupid.

"Okay," I say when he stops in front of me. "Let's try this again. Tell me about Gonzalo Medina."

"I didn't say I know him," he smirks.

I'm getting fucking sick of this piece of shit's attitude. "Seriously, fuckbag?" I pull out my Glock and point it at his head before he even knows what's happening. "Is *this* how you want to do this?"

"Jesus!" he sputters, flinging up his hands in alarm. "Okay, okay, fuck! Yeah. I know him!"

I let him see me relax just slightly. "You seen him lately?"

"Yeah." His eyes shift away from my face. "He was here maybe a week, ten days ago." He starts to lower his arms, but I stop him.

"Keep 'em in the air," I order. "Doing what?"

He risks a shrug. "Doing what guys usually do when they come here. Have a few drinks. Get a lap dance. He may have gone into the back with one of the ladies."

With my other hand, I reach into my pocket for my phone. "You ever see this woman?" I ask, holding it out so he can see the picture of Alix's sister. "With or without Gonzalo?"

He glances at the screen. "Nope. Can't say I recognize her."

"You absolutely sure about that?" I growl. "Because if I find out later that you lied to me, I'm gonna pistol whip that fucking toupee right off your goddamn head."

The man visibly blanches. "I don't *think* I recognize her," he babbles. "I mean, I see a lot of gash around here, ya know? After a while, they all sorta look the same." He looks at the phone again. "Yeah, maybe I do recognize her. I dunno."

"Fuck this," I mutter. "Keep an eye on him." I put away my gun and go back inside, to the corner table where the three working girls are seated.

"Good afternoon, ladies," I greet them. "How y'all doin' today?"

"We're doin' just fine, handsome," a young, curly-haired bottle blond drawls, giving me a smile and a wink. "You fellas here for some fun?"

"Not today. Got a little favor to ask you." I hold out my phone so they can see. "Any of you three ladies recognize this woman?"

The middle one frowns a bit, then nods. "Yeah. She was in here a couple of days ago. With one of Tony's friends."

"Tony's the owner?"

"Uh-huh." The woman wrinkles her nose. "She looked kind of out of it."

"Out of it? Like on drugs?"

She nods. "Like she wasn't really sure what was going on, to be honest. She was barely standing upright. At the time, I was just shaking my head." She looks at me, concern in her eyes. "You trying to find her?"

"Yeah."

"I thought maybe the guy she was with was her pimp at first, or something. It looked like to me he was trying to get Tony to hire her as a dancer."

Anger rises up like a ball of fire inside me, but I keep my face neutral. "Is that right?" I say mildly. "See, that's kind of funny. Because Tony told me he'd never seen her before."

"He's lying, then." Her lip curls. "He totally saw her."

"Thank you, ladies." I give them a tight grin. "It's been a pleasure."

"Come back sometime when you're looking for a little fun," the blond winks at me. The woman next to her nods and licks her lips.

I go back to my brothers, who are surrounding an increasingly agitated-looking Tony. "So. It turns out, our friend here lied to us," I say conversationally. "Those three women at that table inside confirmed Gonzalo was in here a couple days ago with our target."

Thorn clicks his tongue in disapproval. "That was a very bad idea, now. How can we be friends if you lie to us, brother?"

"I'm sorry!" Tony stammers, looking wildly at each of our faces in turn. "Look, I was just trying to protect a friend! You guys are big on loyalty, right?"

Hawk shakes his head sadly. "Not when it means lying to an outlaw, son. Bad fuckin' idea, like my brother here says."

"And seeing as how you lied to us once, now we can't be sure you won't lie to us again if we make you promise not to tell your buddy Gonzalo we stopped by," I tell him.

"Shit!" he cries, his eyes growing wide with fear. "I promise! I promise! I won't tell him a thing! He's not even that good a friend!"

Bullet snorts. "Loyalty," he mutters, disgusted.

"Take him," I say. Before he can react, Hawk and Bullet have him by the arms and are hauling him toward the pickup. Tony starts screaming and thrashing, trying to get away, but Hawk puts an end to that by giving him a hard elbow to the face.

"Take our friend someplace secluded," I tell Thorn. "Work on him for a while. See if he gives up anything actionable. I'm going back to Tanner Springs, to work on getting more intel from Tweak on where Gonzalo and his crew have their HQ. I'll have Rock or Angel call the Death Devils and ask them if they can store Tony for us for a while once you're done with him."

"Yeh. Understood."

"Good." I glance back at Maverick's. "And tell the bartender that Tony had to go run an errand. Let him know he'll be gone for a little while."

22
ALIX

Gunner and the others are gone for hours and hours. I'm incredibly grateful to Sydney, who stays with me the whole time. She even manages to make me laugh a few times, in spite of the fact that I'm completely on edge waiting for the men to get back.

Sydney calls one of the other old ladies — apparently, that's what the club calls the wives and long-term girlfriends — to keep us company. Her name is Jenna, and apparently she's with Ghost, the Sergeant at Arms. Jenna's petite, like me, but maybe an inch shorter. She's got straight blond hair, a couple of shades darker than my wavy tresses, and blue eyes to my brown. But other than that, we could be cousins.

Jenna introduces herself to me, and says hello to Sydney and Jewel. "The kids are with the sitter, so I'm here as long as you need me," she says, sliding onto a bar stool.

"Where's Sam?" Sydney asks.

"She's at a shoot. Couldn't get away." Sydney turns to me. "Samantha is Hawk's old lady. She's a photographer. She might show up later if she can manage it."

The three women tell me a little more about themselves as Jewel brings us something a little stronger to drink. I find out that not only is Jenna Ghost's old lady, she's also the sister of Angel, the vice-president of the club. She has two kids with Ghost, a boy named Noah and a girl named Mariana. Sydney blushingly tells me she and Brick don't have any children yet, but that they're trying.

"What about you, Jewel?" I ask the bartender, a tall, pretty woman with honey-colored hair and a wide, open smile. "Are you someone's old lady, too?"

Jewel bursts into peals of laughter. "Hardly," she giggles. "I'm not a club girl, either. I just tend bar here."

"How do you get a job as a bartender for a motorcycle club?" I ask, perplexed. "I mean, I don't imagine they put a help wanted ad in the paper."

Jewel laughs again. "No, not exactly. It's a bit of a long story. I was working at a place in Lincolnville," she says vaguely, and trails off. Jewel's gaze flicks quickly to Jenna. "I was looking for a change of scenery. Ghost and Angel used to come in from time to time. Eventually Angel told me the club was looking for a bartender." She looks around with a shrug. "The rest is history, I guess," she smiles.

I'm curious about what kind of place she was working in

before this, but something in Jewel's manner tells me she'd rather not talk about it anymore. Instead, I take a sip of my drink.

"So, how are you doing, Alix?" Jenna asks me then in a concerned voice. "Sydney told me a little bit about your situation. She said Gunner's helping you look for your missing sister?"

Even though I didn't plan to, I end up telling Jenna, Sydney, and Jewel the whole story about why I'm here. I even tell them that Gunner's been letting me stay at his place, though I leave out the part about us being slightly more than friends. But Sydney doesn't take my silence on the matter sitting down.

"So… what exactly is up between you and Gunner, anyway?" she winks.

"Nothing," I stammer. "I mean, not really. He's just… helping me, like I told you at your coffee shop."

"Uh-huh," she says dismissively, clearly not believing a word I say. "But what you *didn't* tell me was that you're staying at Gunner's *house*. That was important information you left out, girlfriend."

"What's his house like?" Jewel asks with wide eyes. "I can't even imagine."

"It's just… normal," I say. "Nice, actually. It would even be comfortable there, if I wasn't jumping out of my skin with worry."

"So, your sister... do you think something might have happened to her?" Sydney asks, her voice gentle.

"I'm not sure," I say miserably. "We didn't exactly part on the best of terms. She might just have decided she doesn't want to talk to me anymore. But I just have this bad feeling, you know? Like something's wrong. I just want to make sure she's okay. The guy she was with before she left — Gonzalo — he's kind of bad news." My voice shakes a little, and I swallow painfully. "Gunner told me he found out Gonzalo's crowd are heroin dealers. I'm just worried, you know? I'm scared Eden's gotten caught up in something, and she's in over her head."

"Don't worry," Jenna says soothingly. "The Lords will find her. If it's one thing all these men are, it's determined. They'll never stop until they've done what they set out to do."

"Back to Gunner," Jewel begins. The other women laugh. "Sorry, but I have to live vicariously through you ladies." She looks at me with an excited, expectant expression. "How did you meet him?"

"At a biker bar east of here a few days ago. The Smiling Skull."

Jenna nods. "I know that place. What were you doing there?"

"Looking for my sister." I hesitate for a moment. "I went there to confront Gonzalo. Gunner, um, sort of rescued me."

"Wow, and brought you all the way back here?" Sydney

half-whistles and turns to the others. "You must have really made an impression."

"What's he like? You know… when you're alone?" Jewel presses.

"Um, good, but…"

"Finally!" Sydney hoots, clapping her hands. "She admits it!"

"Guys, it's *really* not like that," I protest, feeling the heat rise to my cheeks.

"Apparently, it *really* is!" Jenna laughs, but not unkindly. "Come on, you're among friends here."

"Yeah," Sydney agrees. "*Heather* is nowhere in sight."

I involuntarily grimace at the mention of the bitchy redhead.

"Oh, God, Heather," Jewel groans. "She is the *worst*."

In spite of myself, I can't help but ask about her. "Is it true, what she said?" I begin, half-afraid of the answer. "That she and Gunner have been… *together*?"

"'Together'? God, no," Jenna scoffs. "At least, not like that. Gunner's never given her, or any of the other club who… *girls*… a second glance. Or any other woman, in my experience." She gives me a knowing grin. "Except for you, that is."

Sydney agrees. "Exactly. Girl, he rescued you, and brought you *to his house* to help you find your sister. Sorry, but you are kidding yourself if you don't think he's serious about you."

"But I've only known him a few days," I protest.

"Psh," Sydney scoffs. "When these men know what they want, they go after it. They don't mess around."

My heart leaps at her words, but almost immediately I make myself squash down my hope. I'm sure the women think they're making me feel better, but it's not helping *at all* that they're putting ideas in my head. Especially because I think they're seriously misinterpreting what's going on here. I mean, sure, he clearly likes having sex with me — and our bodies are unusually in tune with each other — and he seems to think I'm easy on the eyes. But to go from that to thinking he's serious about me? I can't imagine that's true. As much as part of me wants to believe it.

The sound of a motorcycle engine getting closer makes Sydney and Jenna turn their heads toward the front door of the clubhouse. "Speak of the devil," Jenna says with a wink as Gunner comes striding in a minute later.

His eyes immediately begin scanning the large room until they lock on me. With a slight nod and a curve of his lip, he starts to walk toward us.

"Ooohh, damn," Jewel murmurs. "If only one of those men would look at *me* like that."

I don't say anything in response, because my insides are already turning to jelly under the heat of Gunner's stare. He's across the room in a couple of seconds. Between my legs, a familiar throbbing begins, so instantaneous I'm almost sure everyone else can see what he's doing to me. I glance away quickly, and try to compose myself.

"Ladies," his deep, sensuous voice greets us. "Thanks for keeping Alix company while we were gone."

"Where are the others?" asks Sydney.

"They're gonna be just a little while longer," Gunner says evenly. "They should be back by the end of the night, though."

Sydney nods. "Well, I think I'll run back to the coffee shop to check on things there, and go on home."

"Thanks for coming to keep me company, Sydney," I say sincerely. "I would have been going crazy here by myself."

"Any time," she smiles at me. "I mean it."

"I think I'll head out, too," Jenna says, rising. "I need to go pick up the kids." She looks at Gunner, then back at me. "We'll leave you two alone to *debrief*," she says, innuendo clear in her voice.

I glance at Gunner to see his reaction, and to my surprise, he's grinning wolfishly. "See you two later."

Jenna turns to the bartender. "See ya, Jewel."

"Bye, girl," Jewel replies, and moves off down the bar.

We watch as Jenna and Sydney walk toward the exit. Gunner turns to me. His eyes are blazing with what I realize is unconcealed lust.

"Come upstairs," he orders.

"Are you going to tell me what happened while you were gone?" I ask, but already I'm getting some other ideas.

"Yeah," he growls, pulling me against him so I can feel the hot, hard length of him. "I'll tell you everything. But first things first."

23
GUNNER

I have to tell Alix what we found out about Gonzalo. But that can wait a few minutes. For right now, the only thing I want to do is give us *both* a few minutes of not thinking about any of this. So that's what I do.

There's a question in her eyes as I take her upstairs. But I think she knows if I'd found Gonzalo or Eden I would have told her straightaway. When she realizes what I have in mind, her eyes grow hooded with desire. When I close the door to the apartment, her body surrenders to mine instantly.

"I haven't done this in days," I growl almost angrily against her neck as I pull her to me.

Alix's muffled giggle turns into a moan at the contact of my mouth on her skin. "It's only been a few hours," she corrects me breathlessly.

"Same thing."

I'm a little rough with her. But I know she likes it that way. I half-throw her down on the bed and she looks up at me and bites her lip, her legs falling open slightly. I already know she'll be wet as hell for me, and my cock is practically ripping through my jeans as I reach for her.

I pull off her jeans first, hearing the fabric tear just a little as I do. Her little gasp of anticipation just about does me in. I know she's ready, so ready, and I can practically hear the sound of her high-pitched whimper as she comes on my cock. The thought makes it pulse almost painfully. Somehow I manage not to rip the rest of her clothes in half as I take them off her. When she's lying naked and ready for me, I stand back up off the bed and yank off my own shirt and pants. I reach for my cock and stroke myself once or twice as I look at her, but I can't go down that road yet or I'll come before I'm ready.

Instead, I lie down on the bed on my back. "Straddle my face."

"What?"

She's shocked, or at least nervous. But I don't have time for that shit. "You heard what I said. You're gonna ride my tongue, babe. Do it, or I'll pull you over here myself."

She knows me well enough to know I'm not going to take no for an answer. Slowly, she does as she's told, and places her knees on either side of my head. I grab her hips and pull her toward me before she has time to resist, then plunge my tongue inside her to taste her sweet juices. Alix gasps again, more loudly, but the gasp turns into a loud moan as I slide my tongue back outside and begin to lap at her pussy.

I'm not sure if she's ever done this before. But it doesn't take long until she's so far gone that she loses all self-consciousness. Her body tenses for a moment, and then she starts moving her hips to meet my tongue, moaning and writhing as I make contact with her hardening clit. I can tell before long that she's already close, so I hold onto her hips tighter so she has to slow down a little. Her breath comes faster and faster as she tries to buck against my mouth. Her juices start to flow, hot against my tongue, and her moans become half-anguished cries as she begs me wordlessly to give her what she needs.

I speed up, licking her harder, my cock so hard I could almost come just from doing this. Her whimpers are so goddamn sexy as she writhes against my mouth. I could listen to them for the rest of my life, knowing I'm the one making her feel this way.

"Don't stop," she whispers. "Oh, God. Gunner…" Her voice comes out ragged. "I'm so close…"

I plunge my tongue inside her one final time, then lap at her with long strokes, teasing her where I know she needs it most. She tenses for just a second. Then her entire body jolts at once, her hips bucking over and over, losing herself in the throes of her orgasm. She's calling my name as she comes. It sounds almost like a prayer.

When she's just over the crest, I grab her hips again and

pull her downward, onto my cock. I thrust up inside her, hit with an almost blinding burst of pleasure all at once. I only manage to last for a few seconds before I'm coming inside her, so hard it's almost painful. Her pussy contracts around me and everything goes blank, the two of us falling together, her clutching at my shoulders, me holding her hips tight against me.

We stay like that for a few minutes, not talking at all. Not wanting to say the words that will bring the world back. Not yet wanting to let it in.

In the silence, all I hear is her breathing, and the rustle of her hair against my chest.

Finally, Alix whispers something, so low I can barely hear her.

"You're going to ruin me for other men, Gunner Storgaard."

In my chest, my heart starts to pound at what I know I'm about to say back.

"That's the idea, darlin'."

"You found people who know Gonzalo?" Alix is asking me. "What did they say?"

We're sitting up in bed, now. We're still naked, but she's got the sheet pulled up around her breasts. Which is probably good, because I won't be able to concentrate on what we're talking about if I can see her tits.

"The other brothers are questioning one of Gonzalo's friends now," I say.

"Questioning?" she asks, raising a brow.

"*Interrogating*," I clarify. "They'll get anything he knows out of him. One way or another. Once they have some information, they'll get hold of me right away."

Alix shudders slightly. "I'm not sure I want to know any more about that."

I nod. "Probably not. But the point is, we're getting closer. Once we have Gonzalo, we'll be able to determine for sure whether he knows where Eden is."

"What if he won't tell you?"

"He will," I growl.

I'll see to it myself. It'll be a fucking joy to beat it out of that motherfucker.

"Why did you come back here alone?" Alix asks then.

"I wanted to see you," I say honestly. "Give you an update on the situation, so you wouldn't be going crazy wondering what was going on."

"You could have done that over the phone," she smirks.

"True. But I couldn't have done *this*," I reply, reaching for her.

"We forgot to use a condom," I tell her. "Again."

"I didn't forget," Alix says breathily. "I... wanted you like that. And besides, I'm on the pill."

"I forgot, then. I didn't even think about it. By the time I was inside you, my dick had taken over." I'm pissed at myself. I don't forget shit like that. I don't need entanglements, and definitely not in the form of a little version of myself running around. But that's twice in a row that it didn't even fucking occur to me to use protection. All I could think about was being inside Alix. Losing myself in her.

I think back to what she said a few minutes ago.

You're going to ruin me for other men, Gunner Storgaard.

I think maybe the feeling's mutual.

"What's this?" Alix asks, grazing a finger lightly over the scar on my leg.

"Bullet hole."

Her eyes widen in shock. "Are you serious?"

"Yeah," I shrug. "It's no big deal. I got shot during a run.

Smiley took care of it."

"Smiley?"

"Yeah. One of the Lords. Charter member." I grin at her reassuringly. "A few stitches and I was good as new."

Alix doesn't say anything for a few moments as she continues to stare at the bullet scar. I let her look. This shit is who I am. It's my life. No use trying to hide it from her.

"There was a woman here at the clubhouse earlier," she says finally. Her voice is soft, troubled. "Heather."

Fuck. I don't even need to ask anything to be pretty sure what Alix is gonna say next.

"She was, uh, kind of a bitch," Alix continues. "She said…"

"Alix." I cut her off before she can go any further. "I'll answer any questions you have. But before I do, I just want you to know something. Heather means not one damn thing to me. Never has, never will." For some reason, I *have* to know that Alix understands this. I can't have her thinking she and Heather are even in the same fucking category. Hell, it's fucked up that Heather would even breathe the same *air* as Alix.

Alix shakes her head a little. "She said the two of you were together. Sydney and Jenna said that wasn't true. But… I want to hear it from you." She looks up at me, her eyes open and vulnerable. "I just want to know," she says, her voice cracking a little. "Whatever the truth is. I just want to know it."

"Babe." I kiss the top of her head. "I won't lie to you. Heather's a club girl. That's what she's here for — because she's got a thing for bikers. The girls are there to scratch an itch when we need it. Yeah, I've…" I stop short of saying *fucked her*. I don't want to see Alix flinch at my bluntness. "It's, uh, happened a few times with her. But not since I met you."

"I know I don't really have the right to ask," she murmurs. "But…"

"You can ask whatever the hell you want." I reach over and lift her chin so she's looking straight into my eyes. "There's nothing between Heather and me." I pause for a second. "And there won't be. I'm done with her. She can't hold a candle to you, Alix. No woman can."

Fuck me. That last part slipped out before I even knew I was going to say it.

It's fucking true, though.

Alix's eyes soften. I bend down and kiss her, deeply. When I break away, we're both breathing hard.

"Can I tell you something?" she whispers.

"Shoot."

"I'm scared."

"Of what?"

"I'm scared to find Eden."

That wasn't what I was expecting at all.

"I thought I was scared I'd *never* find her," she goes on. She sounds so young, suddenly. "That I wouldn't ever know if she needed help. But now, I'm scared of what will happen when we *do* find her. Because what if she laughs? What if she tells me I'm a stupid idiot for thinking she wanted to be found in the first place? What if she tells me to fuck off?" Alix's eyes fill, and tears begin streaming down her face. "I've already lost my mom. If Eden tells me to go to hell, then I've lost my sister, too." When Alix looks up at me now, her face is terrified. "She's the last family I have, Gunner. If she doesn't want me, I'll be all alone."

There's an ache in my throat as I listen to her words. I don't have much in the way of blood family, either — it's just been my ma and me for as long as I can remember. But for *almost* as long as I can remember, I've had the club, too. Smiley taught me how to ride a motorcycle. I started hanging around the Lords when I was a teenager. After my stint in the Marines, I came back and patched into the club. Alone is something I've never been.

Silently, I pull Alix to me, and let her cry. I don't tell her it'll be okay, because I don't know if it will. But there's one thing I do know, deep in my bones. Even though I don't say it.

As long as she wants me to be there for her — Alix won't be alone.

24
GUNNER

Sometime after midnight, I'm woken up by a text from Thorn telling me to call him. I ease out of bed, not wanting to wake Alix, who's snoring softly beside me. Pulling on my jeans, I go downstairs into the main part of the clubhouse.

Evidence of last night's partying is still strewn around the place, from half-drunk bottles of beer and whiskey to a few overturned chairs and other shit lying on the floor. Sarge is asleep on one of the low leather couches. He's got the head of one of the club girls in his lap, who looks like she fell asleep after giving him a blow job. I snort in amusement, and decide to go outside to have a smoke and make the call.

When Thorn answers, it's clear from the highway noises he's on the road. "Mornin', brother," he greets me, as cheerful as ever.

"Fuck morning. It's still the middle of the night," I shoot back. "You got any news for me from that Tony fucker?"

"Yeah." Even through the phone, I can hear the grin on his face. "He talked. Kind of a disappointment, actually. It didn't take very much to break him. Turns out he's kind of a pussy."

I can't help but laugh. "Why am I not surprised?"

"And you were right about the hairpiece. We disposed of that abomination properly, by the way."

"Thank the lord," I say, lighting my smoke. "So, what's the word?"

"We've got the location of where Gonzalo and his crew hang out. We're keepin' Tony on ice for the moment, so he doesn't get any bright ideas about warning Gonzalo that we might be paying him a little visit."

"You have any idea whether Alix's sister is still with him?"

"I think she is." He pauses, for long enough that I start to get pissed.

"Well? Keep going."

"It's pretty bad, brother," Thorn admits. "Turns out, Gonzalo's crew gets their kicks drugging women and usin' them for their own pleasure. Not to mention selling them to their buddies, for cash or in exchange for favors."

"Fucking *hell*. Sex trafficking?"

"Yeh." Thorn blows out a deep breath. "Pretty small operation at the moment, but that's not exactly going to be a consolation to your girl or her sister, is it? When we finally got Tony to start talking, he told us Gonzalo brought the sister to his strip club to get Tony to hire her. But the girl was so drugged up, Tony assumed she was a junkie, so he refused."

Jesus.

"So, you got the location of where Gonzalo's crew is?"

"We got an address. Think we know where they are. I had Bullet drive by it last night to check things out. We didn't want to make a move until we had enough men to blow the place open, in case they got nervous and ran."

"Good plan." I run a hand roughly through my hair. We need to move on this, fast. "Okay, look. The four of you, stay in the area. I'm gonna talk to Rock about this first thing in the morning. I'll want to bring some more men before we go in to get Eden. I'll call you back as soon as I have a plan."

"Understood."

"Thanks, brother."

"No thanks necessary, Gun." He pauses. "Unless you're interested in giving me the secret to beating Beast at arm-wrestling."

In spite of the tension I'm feeling, I burst out laughing. "Not a chance."

"Ah, well. It was worth a try." Thorn hangs up, the sound of his chuckle the last thing I hear before the click.

I'm not about to fall back to sleep at this point. I'm way too keyed up, and I need to think through a strategy for going in and getting Eden from Gonzalo and his crew. So, I go back upstairs and pull on the rest of my clothes in the dark, then head back outside into the cool night.

It's time for a ride.

The noise of my engine cuts through the silence as I ride through the mostly-sleeping town and out onto the highway. It's been a long time since I've ridden at night like this. It's one of my favorite things to do. The moon is full, or close to it, and the sky is cloudless. I could practically ride without headlights, the road is so illuminated by the moonlight.

Riding through the night like this feels timeless, in a way that riding in the day never does. I don't come across a single car for almost an hour. I keep going, barely paying attention to where I'm turning right or left. I avoid the towns, preferring to be alone with my thoughts. Thoughts of Alix. And her sister. And what it will mean when the club has found her and brought her back.

I think about Alix going back to Lynchburg, to her old life.

A life she's told me is practically nonexistent. Everything she had there is mostly gone now. Even her job, she says.

Right now, Alix is at the clubhouse, in my apartment.

Sleeping in my bed. The sheets are warm from her body. Her pillow smells like her hair. In spite of myself, I get hard just thinking about her there, and the ache almost convinces me to turn back around, to wake her up in the night and take her. I know the sounds she'll make. I know how fucking good it will feel when I come inside her.

I don't want to lose that.

Fuck. I'm not going to lose that.

Alix is going to stay here in Tanner Springs. With me. We'll get her sister back here, and then we'll take it from there.

I don't turn the bike around. I keep riding.

And I plan.

* * *

When I get back to the clubhouse, it's after eight in the morning. Sarge has disappeared from the couch where he was sleeping. Some of the club girls are cleaning up the mess from last night. From the kitchen, I can smell the aroma of bacon.

The chapel door is closed, and I can see from the shadow underneath that the light's on. I take a chance that the prez is in there and knock.

"Yeah?" Rock's voice barks from the other side. Steeling myself, I turn the knob and push the door open.

Inside, Rock and Angel are seated at the large table, mugs of coffee in front of them. They look up at the sound of my footsteps. Angel lifts his chin at me.

"Morning, Gun," he murmurs.

"Morning," I say, stepping inside and closing the door behind me. "You mind an interruption? I need to talk to you."

"We're goin' over the details for the next run with the Death Devils," Rock tells me, and motions for me to sit. "Oz needs a few of us to run the gun shipment to his buyers today."

"How many men you need for that?" I ask.

"Shouldn't need more than four or five," Rock answers. "I'm goin' on this one. Figured I'll take Ghost and you, maybe Striker and Brick."

I hesitate. "About that. I got a favor to ask you. To ask the club."

Rock frowns. I know he expected me to agree automatically. Which I should have.

"Yeah?" he scowls. "What's your fuckin' favor?"

I glance over at Angel, hoping he'll back me up. "I need

some men to come with me on a run of my own. Today. It's important. And it's kind of urgent."

Rock's look is sharp, angry. "Why the fuck didn't you come to me about this sooner?"

"I didn't know about it myself until a few hours ago."

Leaning back in my chair, I tell Rock and Angel everything I know, starting from Alix's unexpected appearance at the Smiling Skull, to Thorn's phone call a few hours ago. As I talk, Rock's expression doesn't change. They both ask questions, and I wait for Rock's anger that I've already used the club's resources and men to go after Gonzalo.

When I've finished, I say, "So now that we know where they are, and what's probably happening to Eden, I don't think we should wait any longer before we go in. We're holding Tony so he can't contact Gonzalo, but it's still possible Gonzalo could find out some other way if we don't act now."

"So, this is the sister of the bitch you brought into the clubhouse yesterday?" Rock rumbles.

I know for him it's just a word. But if it was anyone other than my club president calling Alix a bitch, I would leap over this fucking table and beat him so bad it would be the last word he ever said.

"Don't call her that," I rasp the warning, half-rising in my chair. The fury in my tone is just beneath the surface, and I can tell they both hear it. I hope Rock heeds my fucking words. Because prez or not, if he does it again I'm not going to be responsible for what comes next.

"Gun's family," Angel breaks in, his voice loud and firm. "We got your back, brother." Turning to Rock, he continues. "We don't need all the brothers to go on the Death Devils run, like you said. The Lords can spare a few men to go find Gunner's old lady's sister."

"Old lady?" Rock scowls, a little tension easing in his jaw. He looks to me for confirmation. "That true?"

I take a deep breath. "Yeah."

It *is* true. Or as good as true, anyway. Even though Alix and I haven't gotten anywhere near a conversation like that, I know it's coming. She's mine. I think I knew it somewhere down deep even that first night at the Smiling Skull.

"Goddamnit," Rock mutters. "Don't pull shit like this again, Gun. You don't decide what this club does. I do."

"I know." I nod briefly. "It wasn't something I planned."

"How many men you need for this?"

"Thorn, Bullet, Hawk, and Beast are already out there," I say, ignoring the flash of anger in his eyes. "I need three more."

"I'll go," Angel breaks in. "Maybe Tank and Lug Nut?"

Rock frowns darkly at the table, then barks, "Okay." He rises from his chair and walks toward the door. "You keep me in the loop on this," he warns.

"I will."

Then Rock is gone, the door slamming behind him. The echo of his boots retreats into the distance. I stand up myself, and blow out a breath.

"I could use a cup of coffee," I say to Angel nodding toward his mug.

"I'll come with you. I need a refresher."

The two of us head toward the kitchen. "Thanks for helping me out back there, Angel," I mutter.

"What can I say? I'm a fuckin' boy scout."

"Rock doesn't seem too happy about this."

"Yeah, well," he snorts. "Rock and I have had plenty of disagreements. It won't be the first time we've clashed on what the club should be doing."

In the kitchen, Melanie is washing up some breakfast dishes. "Just made some more coffee," she says when she sees us. "Help yourself."

I grab a mug and wait for Angel to refresh his, then fill mine to the brim. We're heading back down the hallway to the main room when I almost bump into Alix as she rounds the corner.

I start to make a joke about how bad she needs coffee to be running like that, but one look at her tells me coffee isn't what she's after.

Alix's face is white as a sheet.

"Gunner," she says in a strangled voice. "It's Eden!"

25
ALIX

My hands are shaking as I hand the phone to Gunner.

His eyes lock onto mine as he listens wordlessly to the voicemail. I close my eyes, knowing what he's about to hear:

"Alix! It's me!" my sister's voice breathes urgently into the phone. She sounds scared but confused, her cadence slower than normal. It's clear she's trying to talk without anyone hearing her. "Please, please, help me! I can't… I don't know where I am, but Gonzalo… oh, my God!"

And then the phone goes dead, the message ended.

"It's definitely her." I say, trying as hard as I can to swallow the lump in my throat and not burst into tears. "She left it last night," I whisper. "I didn't see it until just now."

What I don't say is what *time* she left it.

It would have been right around the time that Gunner and I were making love.

"I tried to call her back just now, as soon as I heard it. But the number just…" My voice cracks. "Just goes straight to voicemail again. Just like before."

"Okay. Okay." Gunner's brow creases intently as he listens to the message a second time. "This is good."

"*Good?*" I cry. "How can it be good?"

"It's good because she said Gonzalo's name," he retorts, grasping me by the arm. "We know where he is, Alix. Or at least where he probably is. And we're pretty sure that's where Eden is, too." He holds up the phone. "This makes it more certain that she's with him."

As scared as I am, I can see that he's right. "You know where he is?" I whisper. "Are you sure?"

"Pretty sure," he nods. "I'm taking some men there this morning. If Eden's there, we'll have her by the end of the day."

"I'm going with you," I say firmly, wiping the tears from my eyes.

"No you're fucking not," Gunner barks, like I knew he would, but I'm not backing down.

"I am!" I half-yell. "You can't stop me from coming with you, Gunner. You can't! I've been waiting for too long! I'll stay out of the club's way, but I'm not going to stay here and just wait again. I can't stand it!"

"Alix, for God's sake, think!" Gunner roars at me. His grip on my arm grows tighter, almost painful. "Do you realize how much more dangerous this will be if we have to protect you as well as Eden? Do you want her safe? Then stay here. I'll send for you as soon as we get her, I promise. But you are not coming with us. It's absolutely out of the question, and that's fucking final, do you understand me?"

Gunner's face is so angry, his expression so intense, that I realize there must be more going on than I thought. I can't imagine why it would be so dangerous for a group of hardened men like the Lords to go in and get Eden from a couple of petty thugs like Gonzalo. Suddenly, I go from frightened to terrified.

"Gunner, what are you hiding from me?" I plead. "What's going on?"

"Nothing. You don't need to know," he snarls. "You just need to back the fuck off and let us handle this."

"No! I won't!" I shake my head furiously. "I refuse to back down until you tell me what's going on. Eden's in more danger than you thought, isn't she?" Gunner's eyes flick away from me, for just a moment, but it's enough. "Gunner, please!" I beg. "Please tell me!"

For a second, I think he's going to refuse again, but I'm not backing down, and I think he knows it. After a few seconds, he sighs and loosens his hold on my arm slightly. "*Fuck*," he spits out angrily. "Okay. Look." He pulls me over to one of the couches. "I'll tell you what I know. If you promise to do what I say afterwards."

I know this is the best deal I'm going to get.

"Okay," I promise. He lets go of my arm and I sit obediently on the edge of the couch, my heart beginning to race.

"We found out from a... business associate of Gonzalo's that his crew is involved in what looks like a sex trafficking ring of some sort," Gunner begins. "It's a still a pretty small-time operation, but from what we know now, it sounds like they're building up a stable of women to pimp out or sell." His eyes meet mine. "We think Eden might be being held captive by them. And drugged up enough to make her unable to resist much."

For a second, his words echo in my brain, but it's like I can't assemble them to make any sense of anything. Eden's being held a *prisoner*? And she might be being drugged, and used for sex? Prostituted — or *worse*?

I stare at Gunner, and my head begins to shake, *no, no,* as the full weight of his words come crashing down on me.

"That's not possible," I whisper, but it's not because I don't believe him — it's because I *can't* believe him. I can't, because it's like if I don't let myself believe it then it can't be true.

"I know this is a lot to hear," Gunner murmurs gravely. "Babe, I'm sorry. I was hoping we were wrong, but now that I've heard your sister's voicemail, I'm pretty sure we need to be ready for the worst when we go in to get her."

"Eden," I choke, my voice breaking. "Oh, my God…"

"We don't know how many men or what kind of weaponry we'll be facing when we get there," Gunner continues, more gently now. "I can't afford to have you come with us, Alix. It's too dangerous. For you, and for Eden. If you want us to get her out of there, you need to let me handle this my way."

Any protest I was about to utter dies in my throat. "Okay," I manage, my voice cracking. I remember the panic in the voicemail she left me last night, and my heart begins to pound. "Oh, my God, Gunner!" I wail, my voice rising. "What's happened to her? What if —?"

"Don't," he cuts me off sharply. "Don't think about that. There's no use torturing yourself with shit we don't know yet, Alix. We'll deal with it once we get Eden out." He takes me by the shoulders and brings his face forward. His eyes meet mine, intense and searching. "We'll deal with it. Okay? Promise me."

"I promise," I say again, but I don't even know what I'm promising at this point.

I let Gunner settle me back onto the couch, my mind reeling. "I'm gonna make a call," he says. "I don't want you waiting here at the clubhouse. You won't be able to relax here. I'm gonna get hold of someone who'll wait with you until we're back."

"Who?" I ask numbly. "Sydney? Jenna?"

"My ma," he responds. "She's a nurse. And from what it sounds like, we may need her help detoxing Eden when we get her back."

26
ALIX

I'm still mostly in a daze as Gunner makes a phone call, comes back to the couch, and leads me outside.

"Let's go, babe," he says as he walks me to my bike. "Ma's home and she says to come on over. You'll be in good hands with her until I get back."

I don't remember much about the ride over to Gunner's mom's house. I couldn't even tell you what side of town it's on. But when he pulls up at a tidy, pale green house with black shutters, a woman in a distressed T-shirt and faded jeans comes out to greet us.

"Hey, baby," the woman says to Gunner, presenting a cheek for her to kiss. "This must be your friend?"

The woman looks like she might be in her mid- to late forties. She's hardly maternal-looking, with an abundance of brown hair shot through with some artfully-placed silver streaks. Despite her casual dress, she's well put-together, and in very good shape.

"This is Alix," Gunner says, nodding toward me. "Alix, this is my ma, Lucy Storgaard."

"Pleased to meet you," I murmur awkwardly. I'm not sure how much Gunner has said to her about why I'm here.

"Oh, let's cut the formal shit," she smirks at me with a knowing look. "Come on honey, let's get you inside. From what Gunner's told me, you've got a lot on your mind, and need a little distraction."

Gunner's mom turns and heads up the sidewalk. When she gets to the front door, she looks back and motions me inside. I glance up at Gunner uncertainly.

"Don't worry, she doesn't bite," he grins. "At least, as far as I know. Smiley might tell you different."

I frown in confusion at his last remark, but before I can ask him what he means Gunner reaches up and cups my chin lightly in his hand. "I'll be back soon, babe. We'll get Eden. You know that, right?"

"Yes," I breathe, trusting him.

"Good." He leans down and brushes my lips with his. "Now get inside. And get ready. Ma's a tornado, but she'll definitely keep your mind off things until we get back."

Reluctantly, I watch Gunner pull away on his bike and go

up the sidewalk to join Lucy. She practically pulls me into the house, and inside of five minutes, I'm sitting at her kitchen table with a sweetened iced tea in front of me. Her dog, a black and white pit bull named Zappa, is sitting expectantly at my feet, like he's waiting for a treat.

"So, honey, how ya holdin' up?" Lucy asks, leaning back in her chair with a look of sympathy in her eyes. "Gunner told me about your sister. You must be pretty worried."

"I am," I admit. Tears sting my eyes, but I force them back down. Beside me, Zappa whimpers in sympathy. I reach down absently and pat him on the head.

"Gunner and the Lords will bring her back," Lucy says with certainty. "You can bank on that. They don't stop until they get what they came for. You'll see."

"I know." I give her a tremulous smile. "Thank you for taking me into your home. Gunner's right — it would have been hard to wait for them to come back all by myself."

"No problem at all, honey." Lucy reaches over and pats my hand. "It'll give me a chance to get to know the woman he's playing hero for."

"He's been really kind to me." Even though I'm not crying, my nose is threatening to run. I sniff once, and Lucy immediately gets up and comes back with a box of Kleenex for me, which I accept gratefully. "I don't know why he's doing all this, but I'm so thankful. I never would have found Eden if it wasn't for him."

"How'd you meet my son?" Lucy asks.

I tell her about going to the Smiling Skull that first night hoping to find Lucy. When I tell her about being drugged by Gonzalo, and Gunner saving me from whatever horrible plans Gonzalo had for me, she starts to smirk. I keep going, explaining how Gunner stayed overnight at the hotel to make sure I was okay, and then how he eventually invited me to come back to his place and use his guest room until I could figure out how to locate my sister. By the time I get done telling her everything, Lucy is shaking her head and actually *laughing*.

"What?" I ask in confusion.

"Good lord," she crows. "Honey, I should have known it the second he called to tell me he needed me to watch over some woman while he went on a run."

"Should have known what?" I can't figure out whether to be angry or not. It feels almost like she's making fun of me, but that's not quite it.

"Should have known you'd gone and roped my boy." When she stops laughing, she takes a deep breath and lets it out with a smile and a sigh. "He's in love with you. That's why he's playing superman."

"No, he's not," I protest, even as my heart leaps. "He just... I don't know. I think he just felt sorry for me."

"That's horse shit," she snorts. "You mean to tell me the two of you have been sleeping in separate bedrooms this whole time like a nun and a priest?"

"Well…" I stare down fixedly at my glass, frozen. Of course Lucy is right about that, but how do I admit it to Gunner's *mother* — even if she already knows? Mortified, I risk a glance back up at her face, and see that she's cocking her head at me, a triumphant look on her face.

"That's what I thought."

"But I mean…" I swallow, and decide to just say it. "Sex isn't *love*, after all."

"Of course not," she agrees. "But do you honestly think Gunner did all of this just so he could get you in the sack?"

No. I know better than that. It's obvious to me that Gunner can get sex whenever he wants. My mind involuntarily turns to Heather, and I resist the urge to grimace in disgust… and jealousy.

"Exactly," Lucy nods, like she can read my mind. "So, what, do you need me to paint a picture for you? My boy's fallen for you. You think he'd do this for any of the bimbos he normally sleeps with?"

I don't know whether to be horrified by Lucy's bluntness, or to be relieved by it. But one thing is certain: she's not about to let me just change the subject. "I don't know," I shrug, my face contorting into a frustrated frown. "I don't know what's going on at all, really. I mean…" I shake my head helplessly. "I was trying to find out from Gonzalo where my sister was, and then all of a sudden this biker was punching him, and then he was telling me I was roofied, and then…" I spread my hands wide. "Here I am. In the middle of all this. Sitting in his mom's kitchen. Waiting for him to save my sister."

"And when he does — when he comes back with her — what then?"

"I don't know. Help Eden. Get her off drugs, if she's on them."

"And what about you and Gunner?" Lucy prompts.

I think back to what Gunner said to me just before he brought me here to Lucy's. Just before he left to go find my sister.

"We'll deal with it once we get Eden out. We'll deal with it. Okay? Promise me."

We.

Maybe Lucy is right. Maybe she sees something I've been afraid to look for.

"I guess," I say slowly, "We'll find out if we're a 'we' or not."

* * *

As non-maternal as Lucy seems, after lunch she surprises the hell out of me by suggesting we bake *cookies* while we wait for Gunner to come back.

"I make a hell of an oatmeal chocolate chip," she tells me as she reaches into a cupboard for the sugar. "Besides, it's too early to start drinking."

She puts me to work sifting the dry ingredients while she mixes the wet. While we do, she talks more about Gunner, at first answering questions I haven't dared to ask.

"It's always just been the two of us," she says as she folds in the oatmeal. "Gunner's dad" — she shrugs — "he's around, somewhere. But the two of us were never *together*. So it's always just been Gunner and me. And the club, eventually. They became his other family, of course. They made a man out of him."

"How did he get involved with the club?"

"Smiley." Lucy stirs the batter and motions me toward a low cupboard, where she keeps the cookie sheets. "He's kinda Gunner's stepdad, even though we never got married."

I remember Gunner mentioning Smiley's name at some point, but not exactly why. "Does Smiley live here, too?" I ask.

Lucy gives a short bark of laughter. "No. Smiley and me, we realized we're better off keeping our own separate residences. The two of us are too pigheaded to live together. But if I *was* gonna live with a man, it would be him." Lucy cuts a glance at me. "Gunner's not much like his father, but he's got a lot of Smiley's best qualities. He's been a good influence on my boy."

Lucy asks me about my family back in Lynchburg. I tell her about my mom, and that Eden's my only immediate family. Her eyes fill with sympathy, and for a moment, neither one of us speaks.

"Well," she says abruptly, and grabs the cookie sheets from me. "We'll get her back, and sorted out. Don't you worry."

We.

It's funny how much I've heard that word in the last few hours. After not hearing or using it for what seems like forever.

The cookies are out of the oven and cooling when there's a rap on the front door. Zappa, who's been snoozing under the kitchen table, jumps up and begins barking and spinning around wildly in a circle.

"Zappa, goddamnit!" Lucy shakes her head good-naturedly at the dog and wipes her hands on a dish towel before going to answer the door, Zappa following close on her heels. From the kitchen, I hear the rumble of a deep male voice, and Lucy's reply. A few seconds later, she comes back in, followed by a solidly built older looking man, with a broad chest, thinning silver hair and a gray beard.

"Alix, honey, this is Smiley," Lucy says.

He nods once at me, a twinkle in his eye. "Hello there,

little lady. Gunner asked me to come over here to keep you two company for a while."

Lucy snorts. "Bullshit. He sent you over here to make sure we stayed put."

"That, too," Smiley grins.

I'm about to say hello to him when I suddenly remember what Gunner told me about Smiley. "You're the one who fixed Gunner's leg when he got shot," I blurt out without thinking. Then I realize there's only one way I could have seen a wound that far up on Gunner's thigh. And that Smiley will know that, too.

He chuckles deep in his throat. "Yeah, that was me. Gunner told you about that, did he?" He gives me a broad wink. "How's that scar healing up, anyway?"

"Um." I start to blush, but then realize that Lucy already knows I'm sleeping with her son. "Good," I admit. "It's not that noticeable, anymore."

"Well, you may as well settle in, Smiley," Lucy tells him, affecting an eye roll but capping it off with an affectionate grin at him. "You want an oatmeal cookie?"

Smiley gives her an eye roll of his own, and snorts as he wanders toward the living room. "Fuck a bunch of cookies. Give mine to the dog. How about a beer instead? It's five o'clock somewhere."

27
GUNNER

As a courtesy and also a heads up, Rock calls Oz and lets him know that eight Lords of Carnage are on their way into Death Devils territory. There's likely to be some bloodshed on Oz's turf, and he needs to be told what's about to happen, and why.

Right after I drop Alix off at Ma's house, I ride back to the clubhouse and set out with Angel, Tank, and Lug Nut. Thorn, Bullet, Hawk, and Beast are already out in Red Hawk, keeping an eye on Gonzalo's hideout from afar. Thorn phones in with periodic updates as we ride. He tells me he's seen a couple people come and go from the address on the edge of Red Hawk. It's a long low building that looks like it might have been a small motel once, that Gonzalo's crew has taken over as their own. Thorn thinks there could be as many as ten or fifteen people in the building, but he can't be sure. "Not counting any women," he adds. "But we need to be prepared to be slightly outnumbered."

"No worries," I growl into my mouthpiece. "We'll have the element of surprise."

The four of us ride in formation until we get to the edge of Red Hawk, and Angel signals to us to pull over off the road at the pre-approved meeting point with Thorn and the others. I text Thorn that we're here. A few minutes later, we hear the unmistakable sound of motorcycle engines on the approach.

As we watch, two familiar bikes pull off the road and stop. Hawk and Beast get off and join the cluster of us, determined expressions on their faces. They're as ready as we are to do this.

"The destination is about three miles up," Hawk tells us, his eyes going to each one of us in turn. "Thorn and Bullet are still in position, watching for any signs of movement. There's a main part of the building that we're seeing men come and go from. But there's also eight individual rooms with their own doors that might be occupied. We haven't seen anyone going in or out of them, but that doesn't mean anything."

Angel nods. "Gunner, Hawk, Beast, and I will take the main area with me. Tank and Lug Nut, you start checking the rooms, together. Thorn and Bullet will remain in position in firing range in case anyone tries to escape. Once we've secured the main area, we'll break off and check the other rooms with you. Everyone good with that?" he asks, turning to me.

"Yeah." I look at the others. "We're looking specifically for this woman," I say, holding out my phone to show them Eden's picture. "But I'm guessing there may be others. It sounds like they may be drugged, and they could be acting erratically. So watch for sudden movements, but be careful not to shoot before you're sure what you're aiming at."

When we're all clear on what we're doing, we get back on the bikes and get back into road formation. Hawk leads us the rest of the way, pulling us around to a deserted parking lot less than a block away but hidden from the hideout. The pickup Thorn and Beast drove here is parked at the edge of the lot, and we pull in behind it.

Hawk and Beast lead us through a deserted alleyway in silence. Around me, I can feel my brothers tensing, mentally preparing for what comes next. About a hundred and fifty feet on, we meet up with Thorn and Bullet, who are crouched silently behind a sagging storage shed. Thorn nods once at us, and then lifts his chin at a building across another parking lot.

This is it.

Just before Angel gives the signal, a movement from the buildings makes us freeze and duck back under cover. From one of the rooms, a large, burly man emerges, locking the door behind him. He climbs into an old Chevy pickup and takes off in the opposite direction from where we're hidden.

"Check that room first," I mutter to Tank and Lug Nut.

All of us look at Angel. He takes one more look toward

the building, and nods at us. It's go time.

I crouch low and run at a fast clip toward the building. Angel, Hawk, and Beast are close behind. Hawk and Beast position themselves on either side of the front door, guns drawn. I reach down and silently try the handle, which is unlocked. I look up at Angel and he lifts his chin just slightly in understanding.

In one motion, I wrench down the door handle and fling open the door. "Don't fuckin' move!" I yell as loud as I can as I burst through the doorway.

The five men inside jump up instantly. Three of them reach for their guns. I choose one and take aim, winging his arm as he reaches behind him. He roars in surprise and pain. His pistol clatters to the floor.

"I FUCKING SAID DON'T FUCKING MOVE!" I shout again. The others raise their hands high in the air as they realize there are four of us training guns on them. I stride over to the first man, who's clutching at his bleeding arm, and kick his pistol toward Angel. For good measure, I clock him across the face with the butt of my gun. He screams and staggers back, falling against a card table, which collapses under him.

Off in the distance, there's a muted thud that sounds like someone kicking open one of the room doors. Bullet moves forward and starts searching each of the men one by one for firearms. I look with disgust at the one now lying on the floor, and turn to the others. "Where the fuck's Gonzalo?" I demand.

"Who the fuck's that?" One of them spits back, but I can tell from the look on his miserable face that he's lying.

"Are you fucking kidding me?" I snarl, and fire a round into his foot. He screams in pain.

"Jesus Christ!" a third one yells. I aim the gun straight at his head. He blanches, and looks like he's about to shit himself.

"Where Gonzalo?" I bark again. "You wanna be the first fatality?"

"He's in one of the rooms," he manages to stammer. "He..."

A shot rings out somewhere else in the building. "Fuck," I rasp, instantly thinking of Eden.

Angel glances at me. "We got these guys," he says. "Take Thorn and Bullet and go find her."

I do as he says, bursting through the door and yelling for the two men to follow me. They cross the small parking lot and together we round the side of the building where the doors to the rooms are. By now, three of the rooms are open, their doors standing wide to show that Tank and Lug Nut have cleared them. I try the knob of the first one I come to, but it's locked, so I kick it open. It's a shitty, dingy place that reminds me of the motel Alix was staying in that first night, only about a hundred times worse. The room looks empty as far as I can tell.

"Clear it," I nod to Beast, and go on to the next room. This time, I don't bother checking the lock, I just raise the heel of my boot and drive it against the thin wood close to the jamb.

Inside, on a low-slung bed with a sagging mattress, a single figure lies prone. Her dark, stringy hair is splayed out against a flat, dirty pillow. She's dressed in a short, revealing skirt and a tiny crop top. The sexy clothes would be almost funny on her if they weren't so goddamn sad.

I take a step forward, thinking at first that she's asleep, but the girl's eyes are wide open. She's breathing kind of quickly, her chest rising and falling like a small animal's.

Though she looks almost nothing like the photo Alix gave me, I still recognize her.

"Eden?" I murmur.

The eyes flick toward me. Her pupils are like pinpoints. When she sees me, an expression of fear mixed with resignation settles across her features. She closes her eyes. Her breathing speeds up a little bit.

I glance down at her arms, seeing what the telltale marks. "Eden? I'm not gonna hurt you," I say in a low, reassuring voice. "I'm here to get you out of here."

She opens her eyes again. The expression doesn't change. I don't think she believes me.

"Your sister sent me," I continue. "Alix."

She frowns slightly. It looks like it's taking her a supreme effort to make her facial muscles work. "Alix?" she repeats uncomprehendingly.

"Yes. Alix." I pause. "She got your phone call. She sent me to rescue you."

A small sigh escapes her lips. Her face muscles relax slightly. "Alix," she says again.

"Come on, Eden," I croon, taking a slow step forward so I won't scare her. "Let's get you out of here."

As I move to the mattress to scoop up her small, thin form, I hear another gunshot, and then another. I don't let myself worry about who's doing the shooting. I have confidence in my brothers. Eden lets me help her up without complaint. She smells slightly sour, like old sweat and vinegar.

"Where's Alix?" she mutters, her head lolling to one side.

"I'm taking you to her," I promise her. "Don't worry. Just help me out by putting one foot in front of the other, and we'll get you there. Okay?"

"'Kay," she slurs.

I half-carry Eden out into the sunlight. Looking to the left, I see that the last door has been kicked in. Lug Nut is at the far end, and when he sees me he comes jogging toward us.

"That her?" he asks, giving her a long look.

I nod. "Yup."

"Good deal," he says simply. "She okay?"

"No," I tell him, "but she will be."

Lug Nut looks back at the other rooms. "There's two more girls here. All the rooms lock from the outside. Looks like they were planning to fill them up and keep the girls like slaves." His face contorts into a mask of disgust. "We found Gonzalo with one of the other girls. He shot Tank in the shoulder, but he'll be okay. Says he can still ride."

"What about Gonzalo?"

He snorts, his expression turning hard and angry

"Pissed himself. He's waiting for you. Second to the last room on this side."

Angel rounds the corner and comes to join us. "You got her?" he asks when he sees Eden.

"Yeah." I look down at Alix's sister, who's barely conscious beside me. "Take her to the truck," I tell Lug Nut. "We need to get her out of here."

"Will do." Lug Nut carefully takes Eden from me, putting his arm one arm under her and lifting her. She looks almost like a child in his arms. Eden rests her head on his chest as he carries her toward the truck. Angel and I watch them go.

"The other girls will need some help," I say to him.

"I've got an extra burner phone," Angel says. "When we're out of range, I'll make a call to the police and tell them to come get the girls and arrest the others."

"Tell Thorn to take my bike back," I say to Angel. "I'm gonna ride in the truck with Eden."

Beast emerges from the last room and heads toward us. "We better get out of here. Too many gun shots. People will be getting curious."

"Yeah. Better get going." Angel starts back toward the main room of the building to round everyone up.

"Yup." I turn toward the second to the last room on this side. The door is shut. "Be along in a second. I gotta pay Gonzalo a visit first."

Gonzalo remembered me right away. He shit himself when he saw me.

I'll never tell Alix what I did to Gonzalo. Or Eden, for that matter. All they'll ever know is that he's gone, and that he'll never hurt either one of them, or any woman, again. And that's all they *need* to know.

Alix doesn't need to hear that shit. She's *good*. She's a breath of fresh air in a dingy dive bar. A ray of light in a dark, ugly world. It's my job to protect her from the ugliness.

Felt good, though.

When I get to the truck, I see that it's Lug Nut and not Bullet behind the wheel.

"Bullet's takin' my bike back for me," he says. I don't ask, and he doesn't elaborate.

On the way back to Tanner Springs, Eden nods out in the back seat of the truck's super cab. As Lug Nut drives, he looks back at her from time to time in the rear view mirror.

"She's pretty young to be going through this," he says at one point.

"Yeah, she is."

"Your ma gonna help her through it?" he asks me.

"Yeah."

He waits a beat before answering. "My brother was hooked on that shit," he eventually murmurs. "Worst thing about addiction's the psychological pull." He glances at me. "She's gonna need all the help she can get."

"She'll get it," I assure him.

"Let me know if you need me," Lug Nut continues. "I can come over. Keep an eye on her, if you need."

"I appreciate that brother." I clap a hand on his shoulder,

then pull out my phone and place a call.

"Smiley?" I say when he picks up. "She's in pretty rough shape, but we got her. Hooked on junk. You're gonna have to patch up Tank's shoulder when we get back, too. Grab Alix and my ma and meet us at the clubhouse."

28
ALIX

Smiley takes a single phone call in the middle of the afternoon. About an hour later, I see him and Lucy talking in the kitchen for a few minutes in hushed tones.

"What?" I demand as soon as Lucy walks back out into the living room. "Tell me what's going on?"

"They've got Eden," Lucy says, coming to sit down on the couch beside me. "They just got back into town. They're at the clubhouse now."

"Oh my God!" I cry, my hand covering my mouth, dizzy with relief. "Is she okay?"

"She will be," Lucy says vaguely.

"What? Is she hurt?" My voice comes out high-pitched, desperate.

"No," she says, her voice gentle. She puts a calming hand on mine. "No, honey. She's gonna be just fine."

The three of us take Lucy's car to the clubhouse. My fists are clenched so tight in anticipation that the nails bite into my palms. "We'll be there soon," Lucy comforts, reading my thoughts, looking back at me with a kind smile.

When Smiley turns into the lot, I'm out of the car before he's even thrown it into park. Gunner's outside leaning against the wall, waiting for me.

I race toward him and fling myself into his arms. "Thank you!" I start to cry, my face pressed against his chest.

"Shh, babe, it's okay. It's gonna be okay." He holds me close, rocking me a little back and forth.

"Is she inside?" I ask after a few seconds. "I need to see her!" I pull away and start to take a step toward the door, but Gunner stops me.

"Yeah, babe. She's inside," he nods. His face is grave. "But I want to talk to you a little first."

By now, Smiley and Lucy have come up beside us.

"Is Tank inside?" Smiley asks Gunner, who nods.

"He's waiting for you. Says he ain't too bad. He rode back no problem, so he must be right."

"I'll be the judge of that," Smiley murmurs, and continues

inside.

"Gun," Lucy murmurs, putting a hand on his shoulder. "I'm gonna head into town for some supplies. I'll be back soon."

He seems to know what she means. "Okay. Thanks, Ma. Grab some clothes, too. About Alix's size."

She nods. "Got it."

"What?" I demand as Lucy walks away. I'm sick of not knowing what's going on. "Gunner! What is it?"

Gunner pauses a beat. "When we found your sister," he begins, "she was locked in a room, on a bed. There were track marks on her arms. They've been shooting her up with heroin, Alix. She's gonna have to go through detox."

"Oh my God!" My skin feels like it's gone instantly cold. "But we don't have any money to do that!" I look up at Gunner in horror. "We don't have any insurance, either!"

"I know," he says. I open my mouth to say more, but Gunner stops me. "Don't worry, Alix. It's handled. Ma will take care of her. I've already talked to her about it." He watches Lucy's car as it drives away. "Eden can stay at her place until she gets better. Your sister is gonna need twenty-four hour care from someone who knows what she's doing until the junk is out of her system."

"But..." I start to argue, but the words die in my throat. I can't do this alone. I don't have anywhere to take Eden, I don't have any money, and I wouldn't know what the hell to do anyway. This is something I can't refuse. Eden's life depends on it.

"Thank you," I whisper.

"Shhh." He pulls me to him. "It's okay. We got you."

I start to cry again, leaning against his chest weakly as I let him hold me up. After a minute or so, I take a deep breath and let it out. Pulling away from him, I wipe my eyes with the heels of my hands and look up at him. "Can I see her now?"

"Sure." He takes my hand in his. "She was sleeping when I came out here. If she still is, we shouldn't wake her up. She needs to rest while she can. These next few days, sleep's gonna be hard to come by."

Gunner leads me inside, up the stairs to his apartment. Eden is lying on the bed, mouth open and eyes closed. The one they call Lug Nut is there with her, standing watch over her like a sentinel.

"She's so skinny," I marvel, my voice cracking with emotion. I move closer. Her chest is rising and falling rapidly. She's wearing a tight mini skirt and a tiny top that barely covers her chest, showing her ribs. Her feet are bare, dirty.

"Do you think..." I begin, looking up at the two men. I can't stop myself from asking the question. "Do you think they *used* her?"

Lug Nut's face contorts into a mask of rage, but he

doesn't say anything. Gunner takes a deep breath and exhales. "Yeah. I do." He looks over at my sister's sleeping form. "Hard to say how much of it she'll remember, though." He pulls me closer. "Let's concentrate on getting her off the smack first, babe," he murmurs. "We'll worry about everything else later. Okay?"

I nod, and bury my face in his chest. Right now, having Gunner tell me what to do is exactly what I need.

"Okay," I say.

* * *

Lucy comes back from her trip to pick up supplies, and brings Eden a pair of soft sweatpants and a loose T-shirt to put on. "I got some other stuff for her in the car, too," she says, and orders Gunner and Lug Nut out of the room. "Let's get her changed," she tells me, "and then we'll take her home."

"Thank you for doing this, Lucy," I choke, overcome. She gives me a quick hug.

"Don't mention it, honey. It's the least I can do for Gunner's woman." I don't bother to correct her, because it feels good to hear her call me that. Lucy leans down and gently shakes Eden's shoulder. "Eden, honey, it's time to wake up. Come on, girl."

Eden opens her eyes with difficulty, almost like she's having to pry them open. She stares unfocused at Lucy, then looks over at me. When she realizes who she's seeing, her eyes widen and dart around the room.

"Am I…" she begins, and then stops. "Where? Where am I?"

"You're safe, Eden," I say, sitting down on the bed. I give her a tremulous smile. "You're here with us."

"Where's… Gonzalo?"

"He's gone," I tell her. Eden looks at me searchingly. "I promise."

"I feel a little sick," Eden moans.

"I know, honey," Lucy croons. "We'll get you well again."

Eden's voice grows agitated. "Help me!"

"We will. I promise," I tell her. I'm trying to keep my voice as calm as possible, but my heart is breaking for my sister.

"Who're you?" Eden asks Lucy with a confused frown.

"This is Lucy," I say. "She's a nurse. We're taking you to her place so she can help you. But first, we need to get you changed."

"Gunner's the one who saved you. He's my son," Lucy tells her gently. "And Alix's man."

Eden lets us help her into the T-shirt and sweats. The two of us help her down the stairs to the main floor, where Smiley, Lug Nut, and Gunner are waiting with a group of other men.

"You're the men from the pickup truck," Eden murmurs.

"I'm Gunner," he replies to her. "This is Lug Nut."

"Thank you... for saving me." Eden's eyes flit from one man to the other.

Lug Nut looks down at her. His jaw clenches, his hands curling into tight fists.

"You get better," he says simply. "That's the best thanks you can give us."

Shyly, she meets his gaze. "Okay," she whispers.

Lucy's gentle voice breaks in. "My car's outside. Smiley can drive us."

Gunner pulls me close and kisses the top of my head. He turns to his mother. "I'll follow you on my bike."

Lucy nods. "Come on, darlin'," she says to Eden. "Let's get you home."

29
GUNNER

Ma sets Eden up in the guest room, which is my old bedroom. Smiley and I unload the car. I come back in just as Ma is bringing Alix's sister some toast and Advil.

"This will settle your stomach," she says. Eden tells her she isn't hungry, but Ma's not taking no for an answer.

"You don't think you're hungry, but you need to eat anyway," she admonishes. "You'll feel better, I promise."

Eden more or less obediently takes the pill and picks up a piece of toast from the plate. Ma nods approvingly and leads Alix and me back out into the living room.

"Okay. We're good here. I'm gonna have Gunner take you home for now," she tells Alix, glancing up at me.

"What? No!" Alix shakes her head stubbornly. "Lucy, I can't go anywhere now. Eden needs me!"

"Your sister's gonna need you even more in the coming days," Ma says, her voice firm. "It's better for right now that you not be here. She needs someone to talk her through what's going to happen next, and it's better if it's not family. Smiley will stay here with me tonight, just in case. Go get some rest, and come back tomorrow. We'll take shifts with her until she's better."

"Come on, babe," I murmur, holding out my hand for Alix to take. "Ma's right. I know patience isn't your strong suit, but you're gonna need a lot of it for the next few days."

Alix allows herself to be led out to my bike and gets on behind me. From the front stoop, Ma waves to us both, then goes back inside.

I take Alix back to my place instead of the clubhouse. Once we're inside, I pick her up and carry her wordlessly into my bedroom. I think she's gonna be too emotionally exhausted to do anything but sleep. But when I set her down on the bed, she looks at me with those light brown doe eyes of hers, and I instantly know what she wants.

Alix reaches to cup the rising bulge in my pants. "Please, Gunner," she half-whimpers. "I just need to forget for a while."

Groaning, I pull her into my arms and look down into her fucking gorgeous, fawn-colored eyes. "I can make you forget, babe."

I kiss her, soft at first, but she responds with an urgent

need that matches the one I'm trying to hold back. She clutches at the fabric of my T-shirt, and I let her yank it off me. Her hands roam over the muscles in my chest and arms, almost like she's checking to make sure I'm real. I'm real, all right. I'm here, and I'm hard as hell, and I'm all for her.

Growling with an aching need that I know she feels, too, I strip her down and kick off my jeans. When we're both naked, instinct takes over. We move like our bodies were made for each other. We kiss and bite and lick like it's the last time we'll ever be together. I fuck her like our lives depend on it.

When Alix clings to me and flies over the edge, her channel clutching hard at my aching cock, I finally let myself let go. I come so hard it's like I'm emptying every ounce of myself inside her, joining myself to her until it's impossible to tell where one of us ends and the other begins. And it's still not enough. I still want her. *Need* her. I know it will never be enough.

Afterward, we lie together, my arms holding her tightly to me.

How bad is it going to be?" she asks me in a small voice.

"The first three to four days will probably be the worst," I tell her. She'll find out soon enough anyway. It makes sense to be honest with her, so she knows what's coming. "I'm assuming Eden wasn't using junk until Gonzalo started shooting her up. So she won't have been addicted for very long. She should be detoxed in a week or so."

Saying Gonzalo's name makes bile rise in my throat. Even though he's already dead, I wish I could kill him a second time. Gonzalo Medina and the disgusting trash he ran with will never hurt any woman again, though. The Lords have seen to that.

I shake those thoughts from my head. I need to stay present, for Alix. "Eden will need some help to stay off, though," I continue, reaching up to stroke her hair. "Heroin's a powerful drug. It creates a pull in you that's hard to resist, once you know what it's like. We're gonna need to be strong for her. Until she can be strong for herself."

"Thank you for helping me get her back, Gunner," she says in a small voice. "I know I keep saying it. But thank you."

"Of course, babe." I kiss the top of her head. The familiar scent of her shampoo fills my nostrils.

I'd do anything for you.

I can't imagine not smelling that shampoo scent anymore. I don't even fucking know why, but it gets me every time. It's Alix's smell. I'll have to throw out the fucking pillow she uses after she leaves. If she leaves.

"Alix," I say.

"Can I ask you a favor, Gunner? You've done so much

for me already, but… Can I stay with you just a little longer? Just until Eden's better." Her tone turns apologetic. "Your mom offered, but she really doesn't have the room, with Eden already there."

I'm feeling kind of choked up. I need to say something, but I'm trying to think of the words.

"Yeah. Of course," I say instead. "I just assumed you were gonna stay here."

"Thank you." She reaches over and gently kisses my cheek. "After Eden's… okay," she continues, almost to herself, "I don't know what she'll want to do."

"Patience. Remember?" I tell her. "That's a long way off. A week, at least. And it's gonna be a long week. It's eons away."

"I know."

"Alix."

"Yeah?"

"You saved her. You know that, right?" I turn my head to look at her. "No matter what happens now. What she does. You saved her, from something serious. Whatever happens between you now as sisters, know that. You don't have to feel bad, or guilty, for anything that's happened in the past between you."

"I do." She says it, but I know she doesn't quite believe it.

"I just wonder if she'll want to come back to Lynchburg with me."

Back to Lynchburg. The words feel like a knife going through me.

"What's back in Lynchburg for you, Alix?" I ask gently.

"Nothing, really," she admits with a sigh. "Mom's house is already foreclosed on. I couldn't stop the process if I wanted to, and frankly, I wouldn't have the money to do it anyway. And I lost my job, such as it was, by coming here and taking more time off than my boss let me have. So…" I feel her shrug. "I'll have to start over."

"Then, if there's nothing for you in Virginia," I say, lifting her chin with my finger, "why don't you think about starting over here, instead?"

"You mean, here in Tanner Springs?" she asks uncertainly.

"Yeah," I say. "And here, in my bed."

Alix sits up abruptly. Her eyes go wide and almost wary. "Gunner, what are you saying?" she whispers.

"You know damn well what I'm saying," I retort, my voice gruff with emotion. "Ever since I saw you across the bar telling off a man twice as big and three times as strong as you, I haven't been able to take my goddamn eyes off you. And I've spent every day since trying not to think about what was gonna happen when we got your sister back and it'd be time for you to leave."

I lean in and kiss her hungrily. Just like always, her body responds instantly to mine. I fist my hand in her hair; her tongue twines around mine as she moans into my mouth. When we break apart, we're both breathless.

"Why the fuck would you leave, Alix?" I ask. "I know damn well you don't want to."

"No," she whispers, biting her lip. "I don't."

"Then shut up and stop talking about it," I chuckle, and pull her against me again.

"But... I can't just *live* with you," she protests.

"Dammit, woman," I growl. "Are you gonna fight me on this? Why the fuck not?"

"Because..." She trails off. "I don't know. It's too early? We barely know each other?"

"Are you saying this because you don't want to, or because you think I don't want you here?"

"I'm saying it because..." Alix lets out a shaky breath. "I guess because I'm a little scared."

"Scared of what?" I frown. "Of *me*?"

"Scared that this isn't real," she murmurs. Her eyes grow moist. "That I'll want it too bad, and it'll just... go away. Evaporate. I haven't had anyone to... count on... to care for me… in so long, Gunner. On my own, it's hard but…" She sniffs and swallows painfully. "I'm at least used to it, I guess."

A tear runs down her cheek. I wipe it away with my thumb.

"Babe," I rasp. "I couldn't stop taking care of you if I tried. I didn't even see it happening, but it turns out, I'm in love with you."

"Gunner?" She whispers my name like it's a question. She's looking at me like she can't believe what she's hearing.

I bend down and kiss her again, tenderly. "Yeah, I said it. I love you. And that ain't gonna change."

"I love you, too." Her voice cracks. More tears start to run down her cheeks, but this time she's grinning.

I have to swallow a couple of times before I can talk.

"So, stop worrying about me. About this," I say gruffly, pulling her into my arms. "Let's worry about getting your sister well again. Everything else will sort itself out. Deal?"

She laughs wetly, and snuggles against my chest.

"Deal," she agrees.

30
ALIX

The first few days of Eden's detox process are hard to watch. It's terrible to see my sister this way.

It was probably a good thing that Lucy sent me away at first. To get Eden mentally prepared for everything she was going to go through. And to give me some time to steel myself for it. When Gunner drops me off at Lucy's house the next day on his way to the club's garage, my sister is in the full throes of withdrawal. She's agitated, jittery. On her face is a sheen of sweat. She smells stale, despite the fact that Lucy tells me she took a shower just a few hours ago. She complains that her muscles ache, that her bones hurt.

Eden paces the house, her face ashen and feral. When she's exhausted herself from pacing, she collapses on the bed in Lucy's guest room, tossing and moaning. I sit with her, talking to her in calm tones and telling her how proud I am of her. That it will be over soon. That she'll be fine. I don't know if she believes me.

Sometimes, Eden manages to fall into a restless, fitful doze for an hour or two. I sit with her, in a hard back chair next to the bed, and look around the room. It used to be Gunner's bedroom, and there are traces of his younger self everywhere. Ancient, curling posters of sports stars, motorcycles, and busty women fill the walls. On a shelf above his desk are some books: *Zen and the Art of Motorcycle Maintenance. Lord of the Flies. Ender's Game.* It's strange to think of a young Gunner reading them. A pang seizes my heart with longing to meet that boy I'll never know.

I think Lucy must catch me looking at Gunner's things when I don't notice, because sometimes when Eden's sleeping and we're sitting at the kitchen table, she'll come out with a random story about something Gunner did when he was a boy. The stories make me laugh. I think back to what she said about Gunner falling for me, and marvel that she knew how he felt before I did.

Mother's intuition.

I wonder if my mom would have liked Gunner?

I'd like to think that she would.

* * *

On the fourth day, when Gunner drops me off, Lucy greets me at the door.

"She's taking a shower," she tells me as she lets me inside. "She slept okay last night. I think we're turning the corner."

As soon as Eden comes out of the bathroom, I can see something's changed. She's a little less tremor-y. A little less restless.

The three of us sit in the living room, and watch a stupid movie on TV. Something goofy and funny, to make Eden laugh and distract her. Lucy makes popcorn, and it feels… *okay*. Like we're just three women sitting around watching a dumb comedy for no reason at all. The normalcy makes me want to cry, but I push it down.

After the movie's over, Lucy announces she has to go to the hospital for her shift. "There's plenty of food in the fridge, and leftover lasagne for dinner if you want," she tells us. "Gunner's gonna come over and hang out with you when he's done at the garage for the day."

When Lucy's car engine starts up in the driveway, I look over at my sister and realize this is the first time I've been completely alone with her in years. Since before our mom died.

Suddenly, I have no idea what to say.

"How are you feeling?" I ask.

"Like insects are crawling all over my skin," she admits. "But it's better today."

"Do you want to watch another movie?" I reach for the

remote.

Eden yawns and stretches on the couch. "Maybe in a little while."

"Do you want to go on a walk? Lucy said it's a good idea to get some exercise every day."

She cocks her head, considering. "Yeah. You know? That actually sounds kind of good."

I wait for her as she goes into her room to grab a sweatshirt. It's unseasonably cool today for the end of the summer. When she's ready, the two of us head outside and turn right when we get to the sidewalk.

For a few minutes, neither of us says anything.

Then:

"I never really thanked you."

I don't ask what for. I know what she means, of course.

"It was Gunner, not me," I tell her honestly. "I never would have found you by myself."

"But you *looked*." Eden turns her head toward me. "You *came*."

"I was worried about you."

"I knew that." Eden shoves her hands in the pockets of her sweats. "I knew you were worried. And I didn't care. I told myself you were being ridiculous, because I was fine." A small, strangled sound escapes her throat. "And then, I wasn't."

"Eden," I begin, "I'm so sorr…"

"Alix, no!" she stops short and turns to me. "Please, don't be sorry! My God, what do *you* have to be sorry about? *I'm* the one who should be sorry!" Her face is anguished. "I'm the one who just *left* when Mom got sick. I'm the one who treated her like shit, and then just disappeared." She shakes her head violently. "I thought I fucking hated her. And you." She starts to cry, tears streaming down her face. "But I just hated myself, for being such a piece of shit all the time! I didn't know how to be anything but angry!"

Without even thinking, I put my arms around her. We stand like that, the two of us, on the sidewalk in the middle of a neighborhood we've never been in before. Her weeping against my shoulder, and me just holding her.

Back at Lucy's house, we go out on the back deck. Eden pulls a cigarette out of the pack Lucy gave her and lights it up.

"I couldn't handle it when Mom got sick," she murmurs in a low voice. She's stopped crying now, and her words come out in a tired monotone. It's like she's trying to purge them from her system, just trying to get them all out. "I'd been such a hellion of a daughter for so long — I'd told her I hated her so many times — that it felt like her getting cancer was my fault. My punishment, for treating her like shit."

Eden takes a deep, shaky drag of her cigarette, and blows it out. "I felt like I didn't have the right to be there. To pretend like I cared all along. So I took off. And then I felt even worse. Because I *did* care. But I didn't know how to tell her how sorry I was. How sorry I was that I was such a shitty kid..." A deep sob wrenches from inside her. "And how sorry I was that she was... *dying*..."

Eden bangs her hand angrily on the arm of her chair, hard enough that it has to hurt. It seems like maybe that's what she's going for.

"And now..." She swallows, struggling to speak. "Now I'm never going to get to tell her I'm sorry. It's too late." She closes her eyes against the pain.

"She knew you loved her, Eden," I murmur. "She did. I promise."

"Ever since she died, I've *hated* myself." Eden turns to me. A grimace of self-loathing distorts her delicate features. "Hate. I *wanted* bad things to happen to me. Hell, I think I was *hoping* something terrible would happen, to punish me." She stabs her cigarette out angrily on the ashtray next to her and starts to cry again, in terrible, hitching breaths. "But God, Alix, it was so terrible!"

She buries her face in her hands, her thin shoulders shaking. I scoot my chair closer to hers and wrap my arm around her.

"I know," I murmur, even though I don't. Not really. I can't possibly know how awful the last weeks have been for her.

I don't know how long we stay like that. Eventually, Eden's crying slows.

"When I called you the one time — when I left the message," she tells me, looking down at her shaking hands, "it was the first time I was sober enough to function well enough to do it. But Gonzalo found me. He took the phone and smashed it."

"Thank you for calling me," I murmur. "You might not believe it, but it was hugely important. Knowing you wanted to be found. It helped us."

"There's lots of stuff that I don't even remember," she says in a horrified whisper. "With Gonzalo. And the others. Stuff that I think happened, but I can't be sure."

I wait to see if there's more she wants to say. But she goes silent.

"You know, Eden," I begin after a moment. "You know what the best possible thing you could do for Mom is? Know she would want you to be happy. She would forgive you in a heartbeat." I pause. "And she would want you to forgive yourself."

For a second, she doesn't answer.

"I know," she whispers. "But it's hard."

"I know," I say back.

We just sit there for a while, neither of us talking. Eden lights another cigarette, and smokes it.

"Wanna go in?" I ask when she's finished.

"Sure." She pauses. "We could watch another movie, if you want."

"Good idea."

We go back into the living room. I flip through the options on the screen, and we argue over the selections. For a moment, it's like we're just two normal sisters again.

I'll take that moment. And file it away with the others.

Someday, maybe there will be a lot of them.

We finally settle on a romantic comedy neither of us has seen before. As I press play, Eden looks over at me with a tremulous smile.

"Mom would be happy to know we were together again."

"Yes," I answer softly. "She sure would."

31
GUNNER

Eden eventually turns a corner in her recovery. One night, I go to pick up Alix after my mom gets back from her shift at the hospital. The two sisters are huddled together on the couch, watching a horror movie. Alix jumps up when I walk through the door, pausing the movie to come and give me a kiss hello.

From the couch, Eden gives me a shy smile. "Hi," she says.

"How you doing?"

"Better," she nods. "Thanks."

The way she's looking at me, eyes wide and intense, it's clear that she's thanking me for more than just asking about her health. It's the first time the two of us have really spoken since we brought her here to Ma's house.

"Lug Nut was asking about you today," I tell her casually. It's true. Lug Nut has mentioned Eden a few times since the day we got her out of Gonzalo's clutches. If I didn't know better, I'd think maybe he has kind of a thing for her.

"He was?" Eden's face is a mix of embarrassment and curiosity.

"Yeah." I flash her a grin. "He'll be happy to hear you're doing so well."

"She is, isn't she?" Alix says proudly. Her arms are wrapped around my waist.

I kiss her forehead. "She is indeed."

Ma comes out from the kitchen. "Okay, you two go on home now. Eden needs to get her rest, and Alix does, too. I have another shift tomorrow."

"You two don't have to watch over me every minute, you know," Eden fake-pouts, but it's clear she's not serious.

"We're not watching over you," Alix admonishes her. "We're fighting for the pleasure of your company."

Eden rolls her eyes. "Yeah, right."

It's so typically sister-like that I almost don't pay attention to how remarkable it is that Eden is just joking around like this. And then it hits me again that she's detoxing from fucking heroin.

Maybe — just maybe, I think — everything's gonna be okay between Alix and Eden.

I want Alix to have a sister again. I want *both* of them to have this.

"Well," says Alix, yawning and giving my waist a squeeze. "Okay, then. I'm beat. Take me home, handsome."

I can't help but laugh. "Whatever you say, babe."

We ride home, with her pressed against my back. Even though we're both tired, she makes a show of stripping off her clothes for me, and squeals with laughter when I lunge across the room and grab her. I lie back and pull her down so she's straddling me, watching how fucking gorgeous she is while she rides me. We come together, her eyes never leaving mine. Afterwards, she's asleep in thirty seconds, snoring softly in my arms.

That snore, I decide, is one of my favorite sounds in the whole damn world.

* * *

The next day, Alix asks me to take her to Sydney's coffee shop before I drop her off at Ma's.

"I am *dead* tired," she says dramatically as we leave the house. "And I am in dire need of a fancy coffee drink."

"You're gonna have to have superior balancing skills to carry that coffee all the way to Ma's house," I point out.

"I trust you to drive slowly and avoid the potholes," she retorts saucily. "After all, you're the one I'm gonna spill it on if you don't."

When we get to the Golden Cup, I climb off the bike and go in with her, to say a quick hello to Sydney. It's a busy morning at the shop, and almost all the tables full. Young people sit in front of laptops, with earbuds cloistering them from the world. Pairs and trios of middle-aged women chat in front of steaming beverages and plates of pastries.

At the counter, Sydney is scrawling something on a small poster with a black marker.

"Hey, you two!" she calls when she sees us. "What are you doing here?"

"I am in desperate need of caffeination," Alix informs her. "Please, a latte before I collapse."

"Coming up." Sydney looks at me. "Anything for you, Gun?"

"Nah," I shake my head. "I'm gonna need both hands. I've been informed that my job is to drive smoothly enough that she doesn't spill her drink and burn the shit out of me."

"Good point," Sydney winks, and turns to the espresso maker.

"What's this?" Alix asks, pointing to the poster Sydney was writing on. She holds it up and shows it to me: *Help wanted*. "Are you hiring?"

"Yeah," Sydney answers, filling the little espresso deal with coffee grounds and fitting it snugly in its slot. "Two of my baristas graduated high school a couple of months ago. They'll be leaving for college soon." She shrugs. "I'm looking for a couple part-timers or one full-timer to replace them."

Alix glances quickly at me, then back at her. "How do you feel about hiring an out of work grocery store cashier?" she smirks.

Sydney stops what she's doing, her face breaking into a wide grin. "So… You're planning on sticking around for a while, then?"

I throw a possessive arm around Alix. "Looks that way," I say.

"Well, damn." Sydney puts her hands on her hips. "This *is* a good thing. And not exactly unexpected. I'd hire you in a heartbeat doll," she nods, turning back to Alix. "But I have to warn you, the pay's not great."

"Well…" Alix pretends to consider. "It's probably better than the *zero* dollars I'm making right now, so I'm not exactly in a position to negotiate."

Sydney snorts. "Can you work afternoons and weekends?"

"Uh… I'll have to check my *very busy* schedule. But yeah," Alix nods. "I'm pretty wide open."

Sydney starts to laugh. Momentarily abandoning the coffee drink she's making, she grabs the sign from Alix's hands and rips it up with a flourish.

"Done," she says, tossing the pieces in the trash. "You're hired."

Alix is fucking *jubilant* that she has a job.

To be honest, so am I.

Because it means she's serious about staying.

"I know this is just for now," she says, kissing me as we get on the bike in front of Sydney's shop. "But it's a start."

"Babe, you are gonna kill it," I tell her. "You're gonna be the best damn… what do they call it? Barista? The best damn barista Tanner Springs has ever seen."

And I'm not even kidding. I don't doubt for a second that Alix will be really good at this. If there's one thing I know about her, it's that she's determined. She's had a lot to deal with in her short life. And through it all, she's managed to just keep going, no matter what the odds are. This job's only a start, but it's a foothold. Into a new life, and a new chapter, that she gets to write for herself. She has her sister with her again. She'll have a new friend in Sydney.

And she has me.

We manage not to spill the coffee on our way over to Ma's house. Alix hands me the cup and hops off the bike, then takes it back from me.

"I'm gonna miss you," she whispers as she leans forward to kiss me. "All day."

"Me, too," I growl. "We'll make up for it tonight when I come to pick you up."

"Promise?"

"You bet I do." I reach around and cup her ass, pulling her toward me roughly. She squeals and hold out the coffee drink so it doesn't spill on my leg.

"Hey," Ma calls from the front door. "Stop molesting the help and let her get in here."

"Sorry!" I call back. "Okay, I gotta go before she comes out here with a baseball bat and assaults me."

Alix grins. "We can pick up where we left off later," she murmurs with a wink.

I give her a final kiss, catching her lower lip between my teeth, then let her go. "I'm counting on it, babe."

On my way over to the garage, I think back to the night when Alix told me in a moment of sadness how badly she wanted to find Eden, but how scared she was, too. Because she was afraid that if Eden didn't want her help, the last of Alix's family would slip away from her and she'd be alone.

Now Eden's back in the picture, and they're mending their relationship. And if I have anything to say about it, Alix's family is gonna include me, and everyone that comes with me. My ma. The club. All those people will have Alix's back from now on.

She won't have to face everything by herself anymore.

And most of all, I'm gonna make it my goddamn life's mission to make sure Alix Cousins is surrounded by happiness. And that she knows, every second of every day, she's got a man who will do anything for her.

As long as I'm alive, she'll never be alone again.

EPILOGUE

ALIX

Two years later

"Has it been long enough yet?"

"I don't know," I say. "I started counting in my head but then I kind of got flustered and lost count."

Eden shakes her head and sighs dramatically. "You know, sis, there's this little invention called a clock that you could use to do that for you."

"Shut up," I toss back. "I'm nervous, okay?"

"It *has* to have been three minutes already," Eden urges. "And the instructions said to read it as soon as possible after the time." She glances toward the bathroom. "Go look at it!"

I stand up shakily from the couch and go down the

hallway. Inside the bathroom, I take a deep breath and pick up the little white stick. Involuntarily, my eyes squeeze shut as I raise it up to my face. I am seriously freaked out. If it's a yes, then *everything* is about to change forever. If it's a no, then I'm afraid I'm gonna start crying with disappointment.

I take another deep breath, let it out slowly, count to three and open my eyes.

It's a yes.

"Oh, my God!" I scream. "Oh, my God!"

"What? *What?*" Eden comes thundering down the hallway.

"I'm pregnant!" I scream, and thrust the stick out at her.

"Okay, one, gross — you peed on that!" she says, recoiling. "But two, *oh, my God,* I'm gonna be an aunt!" she yells, throwing her hands in the air. "Put the gross pee stick down and hug me!"

I start laughing half-hysterically as I toss the test in the sink. Eden flings her arms around me and hugs me so tightly I almost can't breathe. We're both laughing and crying and jumping up and down in place, until Eden bumps her hip on the sink.

"Ow!" she cries out, reaching down to rub her thigh bone. "That hurt. Let's go jump somewhere else."

We go back out to the living room and she grabs my hand

and pulls me down on the couch.

"Holy shit, this is amazing!" she crows. "You're going to name her after me, right?"

I snort loudly. "You know it might not be a girl, right? You really want me to name a boy Eden?"

"No, I suppose not," she frowns. "Besides, having two Edens in the family might get confusing."

"Yeah. And actually," I continue glancing at her, "I was sort of thinking about naming him or her after Mom."

Eden's face grows soft. "Oh, Alix. That's such a good idea."

My throat constricts with emotion. "Thanks," I say, hearing my voice crack a little. "Gunner and I talked about it once, back when we first started thinking about starting a family. We thought maybe Patricia if it's a girl, and Patrick if it's a boy."

"Patricia Storgaard. Patrick Storgaard," Eden muses, testing out the sounds. "That's really nice. What about middle names?"

"Gunner's mom. Lucy for a girl, Lucas for a boy."

Eden reaches over and squeezes my hand. "That's lovely. Mom would love this, you know."

I swallow painfully. "I think so, too."

"Speaking of Gunner, does he know you were thinking you might be pregnant?"

"Not this time," I say, feeling suddenly giddy at the prospect of telling him. "We've had a few false alarms. It started to get kind of depressing, getting all excited and then being let down. I figured I'd wait until I actually had some good news to tell him."

"So he has no idea?" Eden asks, her eyes wide. "He is going to lose his shit!"

I grin at her. "Yeah. He is."

"Does he want a girl or a boy?"

"He'd be fine with either, but you know what? I think he actually wants a little girl."

It's true. Whenever Gunner and I have fantasized about the future, he tends to talk about our baby as a girl. He tells me he wants her to have my eyes, and my smile.

"Gosh, it's gonna be funny to see huge, tattooed Gunner cradling a tiny baby," Eden murmurs, shaking her head. "I can't wait."

My eyes shining, I smile at my sister. "Neither can I," I say. "Neither can I."

Eden takes off for her shift at the coffee shop a couple of

hours later. Sydney hired her when I decided to quit and enroll in school to become an addiction counselor. Eden works part time at the Golden Cup, and part time as a fitness instructor at a local gym. She got into exercise and healthy eating to help her cope after detoxing, and it's become a near obsession with her now. Her eventual goal is to open her own fitness club. But for right now, she's exactly where she needs to be.

When Gunner comes home, I'm finishing up some homework for my ethics and confidentiality class at the kitchen table. The familiar sound of his engine in the driveway makes my stomach flip with excitement, as it always does when I hear it. But today, the excitement's ramped up a notch, and my skin starts to tingle with nervous energy, because I'm about to tell him something he's wanted to hear for the better part of a year.

"Hey, babe," his rumbling voice comes toward me as he walks through the door.

"Hi," I wave to him, pretending to be hard at work and distracted. "How's it going?"

"Good." Gunner bends down and encircles me from behind. His beard grazes my neck as he kisses me, sending a thrill down my spine. "You look like you're in the zone."

"Yeah," I murmur. "I really need to finish this project. The deadline to send it to the professor is midnight tonight." I glance up at him. "Could you take care of making dinner? I set everything out on the counter for you. Just spaghetti."

Spaghetti's our go-to simple dinner. But it's also the first meal I ever made for him, back when he decided to let me stay here in his guest room while I was trying to find Eden.

"Of course," he rumbles. His lips warm against my throat, his beard prickling my skin. It takes everything I have not to moan and reach for him, but that'll ruin my little plan.

"The pot for the water's already on the stove," I tell him. "Just fill it up and put it on to boiling."

For a second, I think he's going to decide to take a shower before he starts the water, like he sometimes does when he gets home from work. I can hardly stand to wait any longer before sharing my news with him, so I actually sigh audibly with relief when he goes to the stove and grabs the pot.

Removing the lid, he picks it up, and frowns when something jangles in the bottom.

"What's this?" he asks, picking up the object. It's a pair of baby booties, with tiny bells on them. Pinned inside one of them is the pregnancy test.

I don't turn around right away. Instead, I subtly angle the darkened screen of my laptop so I can watch his reaction in its reflection.

Gunner stares at the booties. For a moment, he doesn't move at all.

Then the pot clatters loudly as he drops it onto the stove.

Then I'm in the air, in his arms, as he laughs loudly and swings me around.

"You're fucking kidding me," he growls as he pulls me against him.

"I would not joke about that," I laugh, loving how excited he is.

"You're a sneaky little minx, aren't you? How long have you known?"

"Not until this afternoon," I answer. "I wouldn't keep that from you, Gunner. But I've suspected for about the last week. I wanted to be sure before I told you."

He cups my chin and looks deeply into my eyes. He nods, and I know I don't have to explain why.

"Holy shit, I'm gonna be a dad," he rasps.

Laughter bubbles out of me. "Holy shit is right," I agree.

"Looks like we won't have a guest room for much longer." He bends down and kisses me, deep and tender. "You know my mom is gonna lose her mind when she finds out she's gonna be a grandma?"

I nod. "We should wait until I'm a little further along to tell her, though." Lucy has been asking us to give her grandbabies from almost the second after we tied the knot at the courthouse last year. As painful as it is that my own mother won't be here to meet her first grandchild, I'm so thankful that Gunner's mom is such an amazing mother-in-law. And she's going to be an even more amazing grandma.

All evening, Gunner and I talk about baby stuff — from what color to paint the nursery to whether we want to find out the sex of the baby before he or she is born. They're all things we've talked about before. But now that I'm actually pregnant, it's suddenly *real*, not just make-believe. We're going to be parents. Even more than we were before, Gunner and I are a *family*.

And not only that: Our babies will have everything that Eden and I didn't. Not just a mom who loves them, but a dad who will love them fiercely and protect them with his life. And a grandma who dotes on them. And a whole bunch of other kids who'll be like cousins to them as they grow up. Jenna's two kids Mariana and Noah. Samantha and Hawk's boy, Connor. Sydney and Brick's new little baby, Sierra. And all the other children of the Lords of Carnage.

Including Eden's and Lug Nut's, if and when they have children.

Lug Nut — Bryson — fell for Eden not long after he helped Gunner and the others rescue her from Gonzalo and his men. The two of them had to take it slow for a while, because of how damaged Eden was after her ordeal with Gonzalo. But things are good between them now. Solid. Eden just moved in with him, after living at Lucy's place for almost a year, and then getting a studio apartment on her own for a little while so she could know what it was like to live alone.

Eden is fitting right in with the other old ladies of the MC, too. She and Lug Nut aren't married yet, but he proposed to her about a month ago, and Eden said yes right away. He told her he wanted to make sure Eden would know he'd always be there for her.

And apparently, he can't wait to start a family. As soon as Eden's ready, of course.

So, soon enough, my little ones will even have biological cousins of their own. It's more family than I ever thought I'd have in my life.

I can't believe how lucky I am.

Even though the baby isn't even as big as the head of a pin yet, I find myself putting my hand protectively over my stomach all evening. I can hardly believe there's a little life in there. And that it shares half of its genes with my wonderful, strong, sexy husband.

That night in bed, Gunner is so tender with me at first that I have to convince him I won't break just because I'm pregnant.

As our passion mounts, he locks eyes with me. It's so intimate, it takes my breath away. Gunner knows everything about me, inside and out. He knows my body, better than I know it myself. He knows my soul. And most importantly, he knows my heart.

With a final thrust, Gunner buries himself deep inside me, and it's all I need to fly over the edge, calling his name as I do. He tenses and erupts with a shout. As I shake and shudder, his arms envelop me, warm and strong. This man, who saved me once, and who continues to give me everything I've ever wanted. He's all I'll never need.

"I love you, Gunner Storgaard," I whisper, as I lean against his chest. "So, so much."

"I love you, Alix Storgaard," he growls. "Forever."

THE END

BOOKS BY DAPHNE LOVELING

Motorcycle Club Romance

Los Perdidos MC
Fugitives MC
Throttle: A Stepbrother Romance
Rush: A Stone Kings Motorcycle Club Romance
Crash: A Stone Kings Motorcycle Club Romance
Ride: A Stone Kings Motorcycle Club Romance
Stand: A Stone Kings Motorcycle Club Romance
STONE KINGS MOTORCYCLE CLUB: The Complete Collection

GHOST: Lords of Carnage MC
HAWK: Lords of Carnage MC
BRICK: Lords of Carnage MC

Sports Romance

Getting the Down
Snap Count

Paranormal Romance

Untamed Moon

Collections

Daphne's Delights: The Paranormal Collection
Daphne's Delights: The Billionaire Collection

ABOUT THE AUTHOR

Daphne Loveling is a small-town girl who moved to the big city as a young adult in search of adventure. She lives in the American Midwest with her fabulous husband and the two cats who own them.

Someday, she hopes to retire to a sandy beach and continue writing with sand between her toes.

Printed in Great
Britain
by Amazon